W.J. Burley lives with his wife in Holywell, near Newquay, and is a Cornishman born and bred, going back five generations. He started life as an engineer, and later went to Balliol to read zoology as a mature student. On leaving Oxford he went into teaching and, until his recent retirement, was senior biology master in a large mixed grammar school in Newquay. He created Inspector (now Chief Superintendent) Wycliffe in 1966 and has featured him in Cornish detective novels ever since, the series has recently been televised with Jack Shepherd starring in the title role.

WYCLIFFE AND THE SCHOOLGIRLS

'Mr Burley tops his form'
*Guardian*

'Chief Superintendent Wycliffe ingeniously works it out'
*Evening Standard*

'W.J. Burley's best: an absorbing account of an obsessional criminal, a civilised policeman and their eventual meeting. Painstaking detection, lively intuitions and a bang-on display that the modern girl can be as vicious a bully as a victorian schoolboy tyrant – but pays more for it in the end'
*The Times Literary Supplement*

'Suspense s          hroughout'
*Observer R*

'Gripping

*Also by W.J. Burley*

WYCLIFFE AND THE PEA-GREEN BOAT
WYCLIFFE AND THE SCAPEGOAT
WYCLIFFE AND THE BEALES
WYCLIFFE AND THE FOUR JACKS
WYCLIFFE AND THE QUIET VIRGIN
WYCLIFFE'S WILD-GOOSE CHASE
WYCLIFFE AND THE TANGLED WEB
WYCLIFFE AND DEATH IN STANLEY STREET
WYCLIFFE IN PAUL'S COURT
WYCLIFFE AND THE WINSOR BLUE
WYCLIFFE AND THE DEAD FLAUTIST
WYCLIFFE AND THE CYCLE OF DEATH
WYCLIFFE AND THE LAST RITES
WYCLIFFE AND HOW TO KILL A CAT
WYCLIFFE AND THE DUNES MYSTERY
WYCLIFFE AND THE GUILT EDGED ALIBI
WYCLIFFE AND THE THREE-TOED PUSSY
WYCLIFFE AND DEATH IN A SALUBRIOUS PLACE
WYCLIFFE AND THE HOUSE OF FEAR

*and published by Corgi Books*

# WYCLIFFE
# AND THE
# SCHOOLGIRLS

W.J. Burley

**CORGI BOOKS**

# WYCLIFFE AND THE SCHOOLGIRLS
## A CORGI BOOK : 0 552 12805 8

Originally published in Great Britain by Victor Gollancz Ltd

PRINTING HISTORY
Victor Gollancz published 1976
Corgi edition published 1987
Corgi edition reprinted 1991
Corgi edition reprinted 1993
Corgi edition reprinted 1995
Corgi edition reprinted 1996

This book is set in 10/11pt Melior

Corgi Books are published by Transworld Publishers Ltd, 61–63 Uxbridge Road, London W5 5SA, in Australia by Transworld Publishers (Australia) Pty Ltd, 15–25 Helles Avenue, Moorebank, NSW 2170, and in New Zealand by Transworld Publishers (NZ) Ltd, 3 William Pickering Drive, Albany, Auckland.

Printed and bound in Great Britain by Cox & Wyman Ltd, Reading, Berkshire.

# WYCLIFFE AND THE SCHOOLGIRLS

*Prologue among the schoolgirls*

# ELAINE

'I can't eat all that, mum.'

'Of course you can, you need a decent breakfast inside you.'

'I shall be sick on the coach.'

Her mother, a little barrel of a woman in a spotless, white overall, stood over her.

'Be sensible, Elaine, you don't know when you'll get your next meal.'

'But I'm taking a picnic lunch to have on the trip.'

'I mean a proper meal.'

Elaine was fifteen, nearly sixteen, short like her mother but well proportioned. She was dark with large, soft eyes but a straight, determined mouth.

'I hope this Miss Russell isn't going to mind you coming dressed like that.'

'The letter said leisure clothes.'

'But jeans and a T-shirt . . . '

'Mother, I've told you, it's what the other girls are wearing.'

The Bennetts' dining room was little more than a wide passage between the bakery and the shop. At one end a glass door with a pattern of incised stars led into the shop; at the other a plank door, painted green, opened into a little yard which led to the bakehouse. There, with two assistants, her father baked the crusty bread and yeast cakes which were the mainstay of the business. A business prosperous enough to pay Elaine's fees at Bishop Fuller's, a rather exclusive day-school for girls.

The plank door was pushed open and Elaine's father came in carrying a wire tray of bread rolls.

'That makes fourteen dozen, do you think that'll be enough, Dot?'

'There's nine dozen ordered . . . '

The shop, the bakery, their house were all one. Elaine was used to it, she had been brought up in the all-pervading, warm, yeasty atmosphere and rarely noticed it. Her mother looked after the shop with the help of a girl who was not much older than Elaine.

Mr Bennett went through with the bread rolls, came back and lingered. He was as tall and thin as his wife was short and fat and he was dusted all over with flour.

'Well, girl, you'll soon be off. Willie will take you to the school in the van. I've told him to pick you up at twenty to nine.' He stooped and kissed his daughter on the forehead. 'Have a good time and look after your-self.' He slipped two one-pound notes into the waist-band of her jeans.

'Thanks, dad.'

'You spoil her, Sidney!'

'And why not?'

'Well, she's got enough pocket money already.' But Mrs Bennett's plump features were smiling.

At twenty minutes to nine a curly headed youth of nineteen or twenty pushed open the door from the shop and put his head round, 'Your carriage awaits, madam.'

Elaine kissed her mother and went out to the van. Willie followed carrying an enormous hold-all which was almost bursting at the zip.

# ROSALINE

Rosaline Parkin stood with a cup of tea in one hand and a piece of bread-and-jam in the other. She was wearing jeans and a brassiere while her aunt ironed her T-shirt to dry it after a last-minute washing.

'Have you got everything else you want?' Her aunt could not have been more than fifty but her features had long since set in a mould of sadness and resignation. She was pale and she moved with slow deliberation as though any effort taxed her to the limit.

'I packed last night.'

'I suppose you've got enough money?'

'I'll manage.'

The little kitchen was a lean-to, its tiny window looked out on a brick-walled yard and the backs of the houses in the next street. Every minute or two a heavy lorry rumbled down the front street causing the doors and windows to rattle.

Rosaline had the thin, wiry body of a ballet dancer and her skin was white in startling contrast with her mop of jet-black hair. She had high, broad cheek-bones though her face narrowed to a pointed chin giving her a mischievous, elfin look. But her eyes were sullen and her mouth was hard. She had passed the eleven-plus selection test for Cholsey Grammar and she had become friendly with Elaine Bennett through inter-schools hockey. Now they were going on a community holiday with girls from several of the city's schools.

Her aunt finished ironing the shirt and handed it to her; she slipped it on.

'That's it, then. I'll be off.' She picked up a suitcase then dropped it again. 'Christ, I've forgotten my camera!'

'I wish you wouldn't speak like that, Rosaline.'

She dashed upstairs and came down with the camera slung over her shoulder. Her aunt looked at it and shook her head.

'I wish I knew where you got the money to buy that.'

'I worked in the Easter holidays, didn't I?'

'When will you be back?'

'Three weeks, I told you.'

'You'll write?'

'I wouldn't count on it, you know what I am.'

'Have you got your tablets?'

'I haven't had a fit for months.'

'I know that but being away from home . . .'

'Oh, forget it!'

Her aunt followed her to the front door. 'Look after yourself.' She stood watching while her niece walked up the dismal little street to the bus stop on the corner.

## JANE

The kitchen at 37 Oakshott Avenue glowed in the morning sunshine; primrose-yellow walls, white and chromium fittings. The Rendells were at breakfast, seated round a plastic-topped table.

'You'll telephone if there's anything you want, Jane?'

'Yes, mother.'

'Are you sure you've had enough breakfast?'

'I couldn't eat any more.'

'Another cup of coffee?'

'No, thanks.'

'You usually have two cups.'

Jane's father intervened. 'She might not want to, love, going on a long coach trip.'

Jane was small for her age, thin and underdeveloped. She had straight, dark hair and a sad little face which might have been used in an appeal on behalf of deprived children. But with Jane it was heredity, she was like her mother.

'You're sure you've got enough spending money?' Her father was a grave, anxious man, almost morbidly meticulous.

10

'Yes, thank you, daddy.'

Jane went to the School of the Sacred Heart, a Catholic school though the Rendells were not Catholics.

'All the girls come from good homes and the fees are reasonable.'

Jane wore her school uniform, a black blazer with the school badge and a blue and white summer dress.

'The sisters said it would be best to wear school uniform on the trip but to take casual clothes to wear when we get there.'

'We shall miss you, Jane.' Mr Rendell's large hand closed over his daughter's and squeezed affectionately.

'I shall miss you, daddy.'

'Don't make her cry, Jim, she's going to enjoy herself. I've put a dozen postcards in your bag all stamped and addressed. If you haven't got time to write you can always pop one of those in the post.'

'Yes, mother.'

'You'll have Barbara Brooks for company.' Barbara was the only other girl from the School of the Sacred Heart who would be going on the holiday. 'You've always liked Barbara, haven't you?'

'I'll be all right, mother.'

'It's lucky it's a Saturday and that your father can take you to the school. If it had been a weekday we should have needed a taxi.'

It was a strange atmosphere. In the Rendell household nobody ever spoke a harsh word but all three of them seemed to be permanently tense. Harmony on taut strings.

Mr Rendell looked at his watch. 'Twenty-five to. We've got to pick up Barbara so it's time we were going.'

A pale-blue Cortina, six years old but looking like new, stood at the gate. Mr Rendell carried his daughter's case.

'Sure you've got everything?'

11

Mrs Rendeli was crying. She hugged her daughter, clutching at her thin little body.

# SHEILA

The Jukeses lived on a council estate—14 Stoke's Road, in the Cholsey district of the city. Sheila was the youngest of three, her two brothers worked as machinists in a factory where her father was a welder. To everybody's surprise and tolerant amusement, Sheila had passed her eleven-plus test for Cholsey Grammar.

On Saturday mornings it was unusual for anybody to be up before ten or half-past so Sheila had the living room to herself. She was scraping butter on to slices of cut bread and slapping slivers of cooked ham between them. Sheila was plump with a large behind and a prominent bosom. Her jeans did not meet her blouse and a pink roll of flesh bridged the gap. She gathered her sandwiches into a polythene bag and put them in a haversack then she went to the bottom of the stairs.

'Mam!'

'What is it now?'

'I can't find my wedge heels.'

'They're in your wardrobe.'

'No. I've looked.'

Her mother muttered something inaudible.

Sheila went to the open dresser on which china was kept and took down a soup tureen from the top shelf. She lifted the lid and disclosed a number of crumpled one and five-pound notes. She slipped one of the fivers into the pocket of her jeans then, after a moment of hesitation, added three singles. Then she put the tureen back in its place.

There was a sound of footsteps on the stairs and her mother came in. She was Sheila thirty years on, her heavy breasts scarcely concealed by her nightgown, her features almost lost in fat. The first cigarette of the

12

day hung from her lips. She dropped Sheila's wedge heels on the table.

'Where did you find 'em?'

'In the bloody wardrobe where I said. You don't look.' She glanced round the room and yawned. 'Any tea?'

'In the pot, it's not long made.'

Her mother poured herself a cup of tea. 'How you off for money?'

'I took eight quid out of the dish, is that all right?'

'Christ, your father gave you a fiver, you aren't going to the Costa del bloody Sol.'

'It's three weeks, mam.'

Mrs Jukes looked at the clock. 'You'll be late.'

'Tony said he'd take me on his bike.'

'Tony's still in bed.'

Sheila went to the bottom of the stairs and yelled. 'Tony!'

'What is it?'

'You got to take me to the school.'

Eventually Tom came downstairs, his eyes full of sleep, dressed in jeans and a shirt. 'O.K. Let's get it over with.'

Mrs Jukes stood in the doorway in her nightdress to see them off. The bike roared down the road with Sheila bouncing on the back, clinging to her brother with one hand and her haversack with the other.


The coach with twenty-four schoolgirls and a mistress on board sped along the A35. It was a hot, August afternoon but, because it was a Saturday, there was little traffic. Miss Dorothy Russell, thirty-nine years old, sat in front by the driver. She wore a light-blue dress patterned with huge white daisies which confused but did nothing to soften the aggressive angularity of her figure. She had light, brown hair, cut short and kinked at the ends to make it turn inwards; her features were small and sharp and she had a tiny mouth with thin lips.

13

'In a few minutes the old Roman road joins us, the one which led from Isca, that is Exeter, to Durnovaria which was their name for Dorchester.'

The girls looked out on the green landscape of subtle contours and unexpected shadows thinking their own thoughts. In the back seat Rosaline Parkin sat with Sheila Jukes and Elaine Bennett. Rosaline drew surreptitiously on a cigarette and let the smoke trickle slowly from her lips in a thin, grey spiral. Once she passed the cigarette to Elaine who almost gave the game away by a fit of violent coughing. Miss Russell turned round.

'Are you all right, Elaine?'

'Yes, thank you, Miss Russell.'

'She nearly swallowed the hole in her Polo mint,' Rosaline said.

There was a general laugh.

Miss Russell, who had not taught for seventeen years for nothing, remarked that she hoped it wouldn't prove carcinogenic.

'We are staying near Maiden Castle, a famous Iron Age fortress which fell to Vespasian in the first century A.D. Vespasian eventually became emperor.'

'Bully for him!' Rosaline muttered but only loud enough to be heard in the back seats.

Jane, with her friend, Barbara Brooks, sat primly in the seat behind Miss Russell, the only ones in more or less formal dress. Barbara was a complete contrast to Jane, she was pink skinned and she had kept a lot of her puppy fat though a figure was beginning to struggle through. Miss Russell turned to speak to them.

'Have you done the history of the Roman occupation at your school?'

Jane answered. 'No, Miss Russell, we did the eighteenth and nineteenth centuries for 'O' level.'

'But when you were younger, surely . . . '

'Oh, yes, I think we did about it in the third form but I've forgotten.' Jane blushed at the admission.

'You must read it up; Dorset is a most interesting county for that period.'

'Yes, Miss Russell.'

There was a derisive chuckle from further back.

The coach slowed down then turned off the main road into a narrow lane which had passing places at intervals. They jolted along for about half a mile then pulled into a gravelled drive which led to a gaunt, two-storeyed house with a pillared porch from which stucco was peeling.

'Well, girls, this is home for the next three weeks.'

The coach came to a standstill, the driver climbed down. Miss Russell stood while the girls trooped past her and out of the coach to gather in chattering groups on the gravel.

'Looks a crummy joint to me,' Rosaline said. 'God help us if we can't get into Dorchester in the evenings.'

'Get your baggage from the boot of the coach and assemble in the front hall.'

'How far is it?' Elaine asked.

Rosaline's thought had moved on. 'How far is what?'

'Dorchester.'

'Three miles.'

'We could walk, I suppose.'

Rosaline opened her dark eyes wide. 'Listen to the girl! Walk, she says. You should see me. There must be some farm lout or somebody with a car or even a motor bike.' She looked round the deserted countryside with obvious misgivings. 'We shall have to get organised.'

The hall was bare with a floor made of stone flags which extended down a passage on each side of a rather impressive staircase. There was no carpet on the stairs and the treads were badly worn. Miss Russell stood on the third stair to talk to them.

'Well, this is it! I hope that we shall all enjoy the next three weeks. I want us all to get to know each other better and to learn to live together as a community. There are five of the city's schools represented in our

15

party, all day-schools, and we shall probably find by the end of our stay that we have made new friends, had a few corners knocked off and learned something about ourselves.

'There are a few rules which I shall post on the notice board and I want you to keep strictly to them. They are not unreasonable and should not stop you enjoying yourselves.'

'Fat chance!' Sheila Jukes muttered. 'Stuck out here in the bloody wilds. She said it was near the town.'

'Are there any buses into town, Miss Russell?'

'Yes, quite a good service for a rural area. There is a bus stop about a hundred yards beyond the point where we turned off from the main road. But, and I must emphasise this as one of our most important rules, no one goes into town without getting my permission first.'

There was a general groan and Miss Russell moved up another step to command her audience more effectively.

'Quiet, please, girls. I want to give you some more details.

'There are two dormitories and twelve girls will sleep in each. Pamela O'Brien and Rosaline Parkin, will you come here, please?'

A slim girl with red-gold hair and freckles joined Rosaline to stand demurely a step or two below Miss Russell.

'I have a list of girls who will sleep in each dormitory and there will be no changes without my approval. The girls in each dormitory will be answerable to Pamela and Rosaline respectively, not only in the dormitories but in all matters concerning discipline while we are here.' Miss Russell cleared her throat. 'I will post the lists with a copy of the rules on the notice board.'

Miss Russell looked slowly round the group. 'Are there any questions?'

No one spoke.

Miss Russell came down the stairs and went over to the notice board of moth-eaten green baize to pin up the sheets. The girls crowded round to read them.

The dormitories were in the front of the house, each with two tall sash-windows looking out over the Dorset-shire countryside. The ceilings were ornamented with plaster mouldings and the skirtings were almost two feet high.

'Lady Chatterley summons Mellors to her boudoir,' Rosaline said, glancing round at the evidence of former elegance.

'You don't have beds in boudoirs.' Sheila Jukes flopped down on one of the twelve black-iron bed-steads.

'No? You do things your way and I'll do things mine.'

The two girls who had sat so primly on the coach were standing near Rosaline, waiting to be noticed.

'What do you want?'

Once more Jane was the spokesman. 'We want to know which beds we are to have.'

Rosaline looked them over appraisingly. 'Are you the Sacred Heart lot?'

'That's right.'

'Did they tell you to dress like that?'

'They said we should wear school uniform on the trip.'

'Christ!' She glanced along the rows of beds. 'You'd better have the two beds at the end—not that end—by the door. What are you called?'

'I'm Jane Rendell and this is Barbara Brooks.'

Rosaline shrugged. 'Too much for me, I shall call you Buttercup and Daisy.'

They had a meal at six-thirty and when the meal was over Miss Russell said, 'Now you have the rest of the evening to settle in. Bed at ten, lights out at ten-thirty.' She smiled. 'I should like to see Rosaline and Pamela in my room for a few minutes. My room is upstairs on the

17

main corridor and my name is on the door.' She paused for a moment, then added, 'There is a games room at the back of the ground floor next to the showers and toilets.'

'May we go into Dorchester this evening, Miss Russell?'

'Not tonight, Sheila, let's all use tonight to get really settled in.'

Rosaline Parkin, Elaine Bennett and Sheila Jukes had taken possession of beds at the far end of the dormitory. The two girls from the Sacred Heart were at the other end, by the door. They undressed demurely, careful not to expose their bodies while Sheila Jukes stormed about wearing only pyjama trousers and looking for the top.

'Which of you bastards nicked my top?'

At ten-thirty sharp, Rosaline called up the room, 'Put the lights out, Buttercup.'

Jane got out of bed and flicked the two switches leaving the room in darkness except for the pale lights coming in through the tall windows. Five minutes later Miss Russell opened the door.

'That's splendid, all of you; good-night, girls.'

'Good-night, Miss Russell.'

They could hear her footsteps until they stopped at the door of her room.

'All right, Buttercup.'

'What?'

'Put the lights on, you fool, she's gone, hasn't she?'

The trio put a table between the rows of beds and settled down to pontoon.

'Penny points.'

'I haven't got any change.'

'Neither have I.'

'All right, we'll play for matches and settle up in the morning.'

It was the first time Jane and her friend had slept away from home except when they were on holiday

18

with their parents. Jane lay in bed staring up at the elaborately moulded ceiling-rose from which a thin flex dangled absurdly.

Between hands Elaine Bennett said, 'What did she want you and O'Brien for?'

'Pep talk.'

Jukes said, 'And?'

'And nothing as far as I'm concerned. I left O'Brien there. I've had enough of that.' She studied her cards, 'Twist.' She took a card. 'And again.' She took another. 'And again—damn!' She threw her cards down. 'Bust!'

'Enough of what?' Elaine enquired.

'What do you think? Do you want me to draw a map? Our Rusty is one of those. Silly old cow, but I'll fix her.'

'Gosh, I don't think any of ours are like that.'

'Well, we've only got the one and that's enough.' She adopted a grotesque travesty of Miss Russell's speech. ''I want you to think of me as the mother you lost, dear . . .'' Hands like a randy billy goat.'

'Billy goats don't have hands.'

'No? Well, dear, you should know about such things.' Rosaline looked at her watch. 'Are we playing this silly game or going to bed?'

It was after midnight when the lights finally went out and some time later when Jane went to sleep, troubled in her mind.

Next morning, after breakfast, she tapped on Miss Russell's door.

'Come in.'

Miss Russell was standing in front of the dressing table mirror, doing her hair.

'What is it, Jane?'

'There's something I think you should know, Miss Russell. Some of the girls were playing cards last night until twelve o'clock—for money.'

Miss Russell continued back-combing her skimpy hair. 'Rosaline Parkin is in charge of your dormitory, Jane, you should talk to her about it.'

19

'But she was one of the girls playing, Miss Russell.'

Miss Russell put down her comb and came over. 'Now listen to me, Jane. You are here to learn something about living in a community and one of the things you should learn is self-reliance, another is loyalty. If some of the girls were doing what you say they were doing it was very wrong of them. But it is also wrong of you to come tale-bearing to me. Do you understand?'

'Yes, Miss Russell.'

'Then run along.'

As she reached the door Miss Russell called her back. As a good Anglican she had deeply-rooted suspicions of Roman Catholic institutions. 'I expect you are encouraged to do this sort of thing at your school?'

'I don't know, Miss Russell.'

'Well, you certainly will not be popular if you do it here.'

That night when Jane sat on her bed to take off her shoes the head and foot collapsed and she thudded on the floor while the whole dormitory laughed. She realised that Miss Russell had not kept her confidence but she did not suspect that there was worse to come. The next night her bed was soaking wet and she had to double up with her friend, Barbara.

On the fourth day Jane went to see Miss Russell again, this time her lips and her voice were trembling.

'I wanted to ask you if I may change with one of the girls in the other dormitory, Miss Russell.'

'No, Jane, you may not. You started off in a very foolish way and brought on yourself whatever it is that is happening to you now. You must take it in good part and make the best of it. If you start running away from the consequences of your own actions there is no knowing where it will end.'

Miss Russell looked at the thin, anaemic girl with a distaste which she could barely conceal. 'It is for your own good, Jane.'

'Yes, Miss Russell.'

The days were not so bad. They tramped all over Maiden Castle, they made two trips into Dorchester and saw the room where Judge Jeffreys is supposed to have conducted his 'bloody assize', the Shire Hall where the Tolpuddle Martyrs were tried and the County museum.

'We shall come again and devote a whole day to Hardy,' Miss Russell promised.

Pamela O'Brien seemed to take pity on the two girls from the Sacred Heart and made it her business to see that they were included in all that went on. Jane, emboldened by her kindness, confided her troubles but Pamela's response was disappointing.

'Oh, you don't want to worry too much about our Rosie, her bark is worse than her bite. If you put up with it for a bit she'll soon get tired.'

'It's not only her, it's the three of them,' Jane complained.

'Yes, well, they do stick together.'

The remainder of the three weeks stretched ahead interminably. She considered ringing her parents but she knew how upset they would be.

'We've been selfish, Jane, dear. We've kept you too much to ourselves instead of letting you mix with girls of your own age.'

Miss Russell's exercise in communal living had seemed like the answer to their particular need and they had paid the fifteen pounds, which they could ill afford, just as they paid Jane's school fees at the Sacred Heart, to give her the chance to grow up amongst 'nice' girls.

The climax came over the showers. Miss Russell's rules required that the girls should take a shower each morning, one dormitory between seven and seven-thirty and the other between seven-thirty and eight. They alternated on different days. Communal showers, after games, were common-place to the other girls but such thing were unknown at the Sacred Heart and Jane

21

planned with Barbara to get up at six-thirty and so secure their privacy. In fact, Barbara liked her bed too much and so, each morning, in her dressing gown, carrying towel and soap, Jane stole downstairs alone. She was always back in the dormitory by the time the other girls began to stir and it seemed that nobody had noticed.

One morning, a week after their arrival, Jane went down to the showers as usual. Although sunshine was already streaming through the front windows the back of the house was still dimly lit and the whole place was as silent as the grave so that even a creaking stair made a startling noise. She hung up her dressing gown and pyjamas, threw her towel on top, kicked off her slippers and made for the nearest shower. She had just turned the mixing valve when Elaine Bennett dashed through from the direction of the lavatories, snatched up all Jane's things and rushed out leaving the door swinging. Jane was left wet and naked without even a towel. She did not panic but began a systematic search to see if there was anything she could wear or use to dry herself. She found a face-towel which somebody had left behind, dried herself roughly and then used it to cover herself as well as she could. She crept along the passage and up the stairs without meeting anyone until she reached the door of the dormitory.

'Here she is!' Sheila Jukes's voice.

The door was slammed and locked in her face. She could hear them giggling. She was about to try the other dormitory, to ask Pamela O'Brien for help, when Rosaline came sauntering down the corridor, hands in the pockets of her blue, quilted dressing gown, sponge-bag over her arm:

'Hullo, Butters, in trouble?'

She was too near to tears to answer and Rosaline stood, looking at her and smiling. 'Never mind, kid, it's only a joke. Your clothes are in Rusty's room, all you've got to do is to go in and get them.'

'But I can't go in Miss Russell's room like this!'

'Of course you can, she's not there, she's in the staff bathroom and you know how long she takes. Here, I'll come with you.'

A little way from Miss Russell's room Rosaline halted. 'In you go, I'll keep look-out.'

Jane had the door open and was about to go in when Rosaline called, 'Butters!'

She turned and in that instant the camera-flash went off. She gave a little cry and crumpled up where she was, sobbing hysterically.

Rosaline got her back to the dormitory, she was given her clothes and by breakfast time she had recovered sufficiently to go down with the others. In fact she was somewhat relieved, the trio had been nice to her and it seemed at last that she had been forgiven.

The following three days were the pleasantest she had spent since coming to the hostel. As far as she could tell Miss Russell had heard nothing of the incident and it was not referred to again in the dormitory or anywhere else in her hearing. They spent a day at Weymouth where they bathed and, though the weather broke, she enjoyed Miss Russell's conducted tour of the Hardy country. By the time she came down to breakfast on her third Sunday in the hostel she was beginning to feel relaxed and secure.

After breakfast she went, as usual, to look at the notice board and there, in the middle of the board, was an enlargement of the flash-light photograph Rosaline had taken. Standing, holding the knob of the door on which Miss Russell's name was clearly visible, she had half turned to the camera, clutching at the absurd towel with her free hand.

She rushed up to the dormitory only to find another pinned to her locker. They were everywhere, all over the building.

Miss Russell was almost inarticulate with anger. The trio were summoned to her room and interviewed

23

separately while the rest of the girls, including Jane, waited in the dormitories.

Rosaline came back from her interview unruffled.

'What happened?'

'Nothing happened. I said I'd fix her and I have, she's scared out of her tiny mind.'

Jane lay on her bed whimpering while the other girls maintained a deathly silence.

When Jane was called for interview she had a wild hope that she would now be vindicated, seen as the victim of a wicked persecution but the hope soon died. Miss Russell did not give her a chance to open her mouth.

'I do not want to hear anything from you, not one word! If I had the choice I would not have you near me but I have to tell you of the arrangements I have made. In an hour a taxi will arrive to take you to the station in Dorchester where you will be put on a train for home. I have telephoned your parents to expect you. Pamela O'Brien and Joan Simmonds will go with you to the station to see that you get on the train but apart from those two you are to have no contact with any of the girls. You will remain in this room until the taxi arrives and your things will be packed for you.'

# CHAPTER ONE

Three o'clock on a wet January afternoon. Wycliffe sat at his desk reading an article in an old research bulletin: *Electrostatic Detection of Footprints*. The floor is dusted with minute expanded-polystyrene beads then, provided the omens are favourable, the beads which have not fallen on a recent footprint may easily be blown away while those which are in contact with a print remain to tell their tale.

The truth was that he was bored. For several days after Christmas and into the New Year professional crooks seem to call a truce or, perhaps, they are exhausted by their exertions during the great bonanza. Chief Inspector Gill, his deputy, was taking advantage of the situation to have some time off. Wycliffe felt lethargic and disinclined to settle to the routine of paper-work of which there was plenty. For his lethargy he blamed the heating and ventilating system against which he waged constant war.

He got up and went over to the large window which looked out over a dismal landscaped garden to one of the main highways in and out of the city. Double glazing. The damned thing wouldn't even open and the room was very nearly sound proof. Like being in a padded cell.

Outside rain fell vertically out of a leaden sky, cars

trooped nose to tail in ordered lanes, their screen-wipers beating time . . .

'Futile!'

He would have found it difficult to say exactly what it was that struck him as futile; the cars following each other like sheep, his job, or just life.

He was addicted to staring out of windows but from this one there was rarely anything to see but the endless streams of traffic. On a good day he might catch sight of the groundsman clearing litter, weeding or cutting the grass. It was a poor exchange for his old office which had overlooked a small public park where there were mothers and children, lovers and tramps and old gentlemen who each had a special seat on which to sleep in the sunshine. It could not always have been sunny but, in retrospect, it seemed so.

The telephone rang. He sighed and turned back to his desk.

'Wycliffe.'

Sergeant Bourne, his administrative assistant, reported the finding of a body in a flat in one of the new blocks near the city centre.

'Grenville House, sixth floor, a woman dead in suspicious circumstances, sir. The caretaker phoned the local station and they are passing it to us. Inspector Scales is on his way there with D.C. Dixon.'

'What do they mean by "suspicious circumstances"? Why can't they say what they mean?' Wycliffe was irritable.

'Perhaps they're not sure what they mean yet, sir.'

Bourne was good at putting the sting in a soft answer. Anyway it was an excuse to get out of the office.

Grenville House was one of the first fruits of a 'new community policy' for the city centre. Translated, it meant that the council wanted people to go back to live in an area from which the developers had turned them out. Grenville House consisted of fairly expensive flats over shops.

Wycliffe drove slowly in the afternoon traffic. The street lamps were on and, despite the rain, there were crowds of pedestrians milling around between the big stores where the January sales were persuading people to part with the money they had held on to over Christmas.

The entrance to Grenville House was between a furniture shop and a hi-fi establishment. A uniformed constable stepped out of the shelter of the canopied doorway and saluted as Wycliffe parked on the yellow lines.

'Flat 602, sir. Inspector Scales is up there with the doctor.'

The entrance was blue-carpeted, the lift smooth and silent. He got out on the sixth; a carpeted landing with four doors and a corridor with a notice: To Emergency Stairs. The door of 602 was open and in the hall a constable tried to make himself small. A card in a metal frame secured to the door read: Miss Debbie Joyce.

Scales was in the living room, a large room on split levels; up three steps to the dining area and the kitchen beyond. A large window, going almost to the floor, looked out over the grey city which, for the most part, had not yet sprouted above three or four floors. Scales was talking to the doctor who was in shirt sleeves and they broke off as Wycliffe came in. Scales was elegant. Not only was he the best-dressed man in the squad but his manner and general bearing suggested a top-ranking executive rather than a policeman. Wycliffe always felt foolishly diffident about giving him orders.

'She's in the kitchen, sir.'

'The kitchen?'

Few murders are committed in kitchens so if this proved to be murder the case had got off to an unusual start.

Wycliffe shook hands with the doctor, a wizened little man with a swingeing cold. The doctor took out a white handkerchief and blew violently.

'This damned weather!' He rubbed his nose and put the handkerchief away. 'She was strangled but I fancy she was knocked on the head first. She certainly received a blow to the base of her skull. I haven't moved her, of course.'

'Could she have struck her head in falling?'

'Possible, but I don't think so. You'll have to ask Franks when he's taken a look at her.' He sneezed. 'You'll get it all from him.'

'How long has she been dead?'

The doctor shrugged. 'A week? Several days, certainly. There again you'll have to rely on your experts.' He sneezed again. 'You won't want me any more? I've got work to do.'

'No, thank you for your help, doctor. We know where to find you.'

The doctor put on his jacket, picked up his bag and bustled out.

Wycliffe turned to Scales. 'She's been lying in there for a week?'

'It looks like it. The caretaker says she's a singer in the cabaret at the Golden Cockerel—the place in Judson Street.'

'A young woman, then?'

'Early to middle twenties. It's like this, sir: a week ago yesterday she told the caretaker of the flats that the club was closing for ten days for a face-lift and that she was going to London. She said that there was something wrong with her electric cooker and that she had asked the Electricity Board to send a man while she was away. She wanted the caretaker to let the chap in with his pass key. The electrician arrived this afternoon, the caretaker let him in and, together, they found her body.'

Wycliffe went up the three steps to the dining alcove and opened the kitchen door. The nauseating stench of putrefaction halted him for a moment.

'I opened the kitchen window. There seemed no point . . . '

'No, of course not.'

The kitchen was small but well equipped. White fittings with green patterned tiles on floor and walls. The body was lying partly on its right side and partly on the face with the head near the window which had a low sill paved with tiles. Rain spattered on to the sill through the open window. The dead girl wore a snugly fitting black jumper and slacks. She had a mass of black hair which almost hid her face but what he could see of it was livid and becoming bloated. The body was facing an open refrigerator. Fragments of a jug with a floral pattern were scattered for some distance around the body and the floor was stained, presumably where milk had dried on the tiles.

An electric kettle was plugged in but switched off and a teapot with two cups and saucers of the same pattern as the broken jug stood on a tray near the kettle. On the face of it she had been killed while she was making tea.

Wycliffe went back to the living room. 'Where's Dixon?'

'I've sent him to take a statement from the woman next door—604. D.C. Fowler is here too, he's doing the other flats in the building.'

Scales had tipped the contents of the girl's handbag on to the table. A cigarette pack, lighter, compact, lipstick, tissues, thirty-seven pounds in notes and some coin, a cheque book and banker's card. Scales pointed to a key ring with a yellow cockerel on the tab.

Wycliffe knew the club, a canopied entrance with a garish cockerel in neon lights over the door. It had a limited gaming licence and it was a favourite rendezvous for the city's wide boys. The place had been raided more than once but the proprietor, a Maltese called Bourg, was always a jump ahead. Ten to one the girl had got herself mixed up in some sordid

29

intrigue and had tried to be too clever. He imagined a young face framed in that soft, fine, black hair.

'Futile!'

There was a commotion in the hall; Smith, the police photographer, had arrived with his equipment. Sergeant Smith was middle-aged, morose, and a martyr to indigestion. Lean and grey; his hair, his clothes, even his skin were grey. He acknowledged Wycliffe with the minimum of ceremony.

'Where is it?'

Soon he would be grumbling about the stench, the position of the body, the lighting, the space he had to work in and the inadequacy of his equipment but the grumbles were routine and only very new boys took any notice.

Debbie, he supposed, was short for Deborah though mothers are capable of anything. Well, Debbie had been murdered and the professionals, the specialists, were taking over, taking over her body, her flat and, as far as possible, they would take over her life as she had led it up to the moment of her dissolution. There were specialists for everything these days and it was getting worse.

A good witchdoctor could identify, convict and punish the guilty; in his spare time he could restore fertility to crops, cattle and women; treat the diseases of animals and men; drive out devils and make rain. What could he, Detective Chief Superintendent Wycliffe, do? Here at the scene of the crime he was redundant, waiting on his specialists. In fact, if he followed protocol, he would not be here at all, he would be sitting in his hermetically sealed office, sifting through reports, directing, co-ordinating and making more reports . . . To hell with that!

Perhaps he was in for a bout of 'flu, there was a lot of it about.

There was little furniture in the living room, almost everything was built in. A studio couch which looked as though it could also serve as a bed had certainly seen better days. There were two battered easy chairs which did not match and a corner cupboard full of knick-knacks. Apart from a record player and a radio that was all. No pictures on the walls; only professional photographs of Debbie stuck on with sellotape. They were all signed in an affected scrawl, 'Debbie'. Seen full-faced she was broad across the forehead and between her high cheekbones but her face narrowed quickly to a small, pointed chin which gave her a puckish look, mischievous with more than a hint of malice. The photographs showed an evolutionary trend from the all-revealing to the almost total cover-up. Her most recent photographs (they were all dated) showed her in a white gown which swept the floor.

'Franks is taking his time, isn't he?'

'He was at a meeting in the hospital.'

Wycliffe looked round the flat.

In the bedroom there was a travelling case open on the floor by the wardrobe and partly packed. Other items, waiting to be packed, were laid out on the bed and these included a white evening gown in a polythene dust-cover. The bed was double and made up for two. In the wardrobe, hanging with her clothes, he found a man's dressing gown, soiled and shabby with a cigarette burn in the lapel. On the floor of the wardrobe, with a dozen pairs of her shoes, there was a pair of men's slippers, the soles worn through. They were on the small side, six-and-a-half or seven.

From the bedroom he went to the bathroom, the lavatory and he even snooped in a small closet used for storing junk. His impression was one of tattiness and neglect. What furniture there was could have been bought in the nearest sale room. Whatever else Debbie Joyce had been she was not house-proud.

He went back to the living room, lit his pipe and stood, staring out of the window. Night was closing over the city although it was still short of five o'clock.

There was an office block not far away which looked like a layer cake—alternate bands of light and dark. He could see into one large office where rows of girls sat at typewriters, and on another floor men were working at drawing boards clamped in special stands like easels.

At about this time a week ago Debbie Joyce had been in her bedroom packing a case for her trip to London. Somebody had rung the doorbell and she had answered it. Either she knew her visitor or he had told a good enough tale to be invited in and offered a cup of tea. (Wycliffe was quite sure that it was not a woman's crime.) Surely they must have been acquainted, well enough acquainted for the man to have a motive for murder.

She had gone into the kitchen to make tea. Perhaps they continued to talk through the open door; then, quite naturally, he had joined her . . .

Someone she trusted or someone who seemed harmless.

Wycliffe turned away from the window. 'I'll be back.'

Scales smiled. He had worked with Wycliffe for long enough to know his ways.

604 had a card on the door also. Mr and Mrs Gordon Clarke. As Wycliffe was about to ring, the door opened and he was confronted by D.C. Dixon, the youngest of his detectives. Dixon had fair hair and freckles and a seemingly incurable habit of blushing whenever he found himself in any situation in the least degree embarrassing. He blushed now.

'I'm sorry, sir.'

'What for?'

A short, plump woman, fortyish was seeing Dixon out.

'Mrs Clarke?' Wycliffe introduced himself.

'I've just told your young man all I know about it.'

'I'm sure you have but I'd like to ask you a few questions if I may.'

32

She was soft skinned and pink, inclined to wobble like a jelly and, Wycliffe suspected, as likely to laugh as cry. She was not really averse to telling her story again; she would certainly repeat it endlessly to her friends at the hairdresser's and elsewhere.

'My hubby's away a lot, he's a sales rep for Rabat Toiletries—sales manager, really—so I'm often here alone and it's nice to have someone handy who can . . .'

'You were a friend of Miss Joyce?'

'Not exactly a friend, more an acquaintance. Actually you couldn't say that she was a friendly sort of girl. In fact, at first, she was really stand-offish, quite rude, but she soon got over that.'

'Who pays for the flat?'

She chuckled, as though at a risqué joke. 'Oh, so you've tumbled to that already? Well, it's obvious somebody does, isn't it? But I don't know who he is. These flats aren't cheap.' Her baby face became solemn. 'I shouldn't laugh, should I? But it's difficult to realise . . . You think; I've been here all week imagining about her living it up in London and all the time she's been lying there.'

'Have you seen him?'

She looked vague, momentarily. 'Her man, you mean? Oh, yes, I've seen him several times. He's about your age, distinguished-looking.'

'Could be her father.'

'Not on your life! Debbie didn't come out of the top drawer and he did, you can always tell.'

'When have you seen him here?'

'Afternoons. I often go window shopping in the afternoons and twice he's come out of the lift while I've been waiting to go down. I've also passed him two or three times in the vestibule downstairs.'

'Five or six times—in how long?'

'Spread over the eight months since we moved in.'

'Can you describe him?'

33

She screwed up her face. 'He's tall, slim but putting it on a bit round the middle. He's got a big head with tiny features all close together. Funny looking.'

'How does he dress?'

'Very quiet and expensive. Grey; either mottled or with a fine stripe. No hat. Which reminds me, he's sandy haired, going thin.'

'She never mentioned him?'

'Never. She wasn't one for telling you her business.'

'Did she have many visitors?'

'Hardly any. Of course she was working every evening; she'd come home about three in the morning and she wouldn't be up until eleven or twelve . . . you know she worked at the club?'

'The Golden Cockerel, yes, I know. Did she ever bring anybody home with her?'

Mrs Clarke seemed amused. Her manner was arch. 'Well, no, I don't think anybody came home with her.'

Wycliffe almost expected her to pat his knee and say, 'You naughty boy!'

The husband must have done pretty well out of his toiletries. The living room was expensively furnished with a large settee and easy chairs covered with real hide. There was a stereo outfit which looked like something out of science fiction and a gigantic colour television. The colour scheme was old gold from the carpet to the wallpaper, cushions and curtains. Everything was 'to tone' as Mrs Clarke would almost certainly have said. The pictures on the wall were real paintings but he was sure that she had bought them with a piece of curtain material in her hand.

'Tell me about when you last saw her.'

'Well, it was a week ago today, last Monday. She came to lunch as usual, about one . . . '

'You mean that she came in here for lunch?'

'Oh, yes, most days. That's how I came to know her as well as I do. As I said, I'm on my own most of the time and it's nice to have somebody coming in, there's no satisfaction in cooking for one. When I suggested it she wasn't keen but she came round and now she seems to look forward to it—I mean she did.' She was playing with the pendant stone which hung in the plunging V-neck of her woollen dress. 'I don't think the poor girl was very domesticated; if she hadn't come here she would have been eating out of tins.'

'What about the people in the other two flats on this floor?'

She shifted her position and pulled down her dress to within speaking distance of her plump knees. 'Well, there's nobody in 601 most of the time. It belongs to Pneumax Industries and they keep it for visiting executives. In 603 there's a couple with two boys, aged seven and eleven. It's a bigger flat than this. He's the manager of a building society; they're pleasant enough people but when you try to keep your place nice you don't want two boys romping all over it. To be honest, I haven't given Mrs Woodward—that's her name—much encouragement.'

'Did Debbie tell you anything about herself or her family?'

'Practically nothing. She didn't give much away. She did say once that she'd gone to school in the city and that she'd been brought up by a maiden aunt. I can't think of anything else.'

'You must have talked about something.'

She smiled. 'Perhaps I did most of the talking. When she said anything it was usually about the club. She had a way of telling a story—laugh! Yet she hardly fetched a smile. What goes on in those places you'd never believe and Debbie had a wicked way of telling it.'

'You were going to tell me about the last time you saw her.'

'So I was. Well, as I said, she came here to lunch and by the time we'd washed up it must have been after two. She said, "I'd better be getting my skates on, I'm catching the night train and I haven't done a thing about getting ready.'' Of course, I knew the club was closed and that she was going to London for a week.'

'She was going for a week?'

'That's what she said. She told me to expect her back sometime on Monday, that's today. As a matter of fact, I took in extra milk and a loaf of bread for her this morning.'

She reached for a box of cigarettes, offered them to Wycliffe and, when he refused, lit one herself. She held the cigarette awkwardly and the smoke made her cough.

'I don't smoke very often but I need something to settle my nerves.'

'When did you first hear what had happened?'

'When Stebbings, the caretaker, came ringing my doorbell looking as though he was going to pass out. He phoned the doctor from here, nothing would have persuaded him to go back in that flat.'

The light was so dim that it was becoming difficult to see across the room. Her face, as she talked, was a pale blur. He would have liked to switch on the light but he had no reasonable excuse for doing so.

'What did you think of her as a person?'

A mild exclamation of protest. 'That's a question; I don't speak ill of the living let alone the dead.'

'Unless we find out all we can about Debbie Joyce we are unlikely to discover her murderer, Mrs Clarke.'

After a time she allowed herself to be persuaded. 'Well, I must admit that Debbie had a side to her that I didn't like. You got the impression sometimes that she took a delight in hurting people. I suppose you could say that she had a mischievous streak, like people who are always playing practical jokes, but I think there was more to it than that.' She looked at Wycliffe anxiously, fearful that her candour might shock him.

'I can't forget what she told me about the pianist at the club. That really upset me. All he did was to

36

criticise the way she sang one of her songs and she fixed it so that he lost his job, a man with a wife and two children to support.'

'What did she do?'

'Well, they were losing cigarettes from the store and Bourg, the boss, was furious about it. Anyway, Debbie took four hundred cigarettes and hid them in the pianist's locker, then tipped off the boss that they were there.' She broke off genuinely agitated. 'The worst of it was that she seemed proud of what she'd done. "Nobody treads on my neck," that was her favourite expression.'

She was silent for a while, waiting for him to speak, but then she went on, 'I don't want you to think she was always like that, she could be good company and I was glad to have her coming in but she had that other side to her.'

When Wycliffe still did not speak she said, 'Well, I suppose we've all got our faults and our funny ways, but you did ask . . .'

She could not know that Wycliffe was beginning to live a new world, a world which she was helping to create for him, the world of Debbie Joyce.

'You really have been a great help, Mrs Clarke.'

'Have I really?' She seemed pleased and surprised.

Wycliffe returned to the dead girl's flat. The case was getting under way. Inspector Scales had been joined by two more detectives and they were making a thorough search of the flat. Dr Franks, the pathologist, was examining the body prior to its removal to the mortuary and Sergeant Smith was standing by to take more photographs. In an hour or two every detail of the flat and of its contents would have been recorded on film and on paper.

As Wycliffe entered the living room Franks came out of the kitchen.

'Well?' Wycliffe greeted him.

'You can have her moved when you like.'

Franks had worked with Wycliffe so often that they were like members of the same team. They no longer needed to spell out ideas and they could sense each other's doubts and reservations but physically and temperamentally they could hardly have been less alike. The pathologist was stout, pink and shining like a precocious baby fresh from his bath. He was invincibly cheerful, he accepted things as he found them and seemed utterly lacking in any desire to change either himself or his world. By comparison, Wycliffe seemed, to himself at least, tentative, often self-conscious and given to needless worry. He was certainly aware of his own defects and frequently discouraged by the world about him.

Franks made his preliminary report.

'She died of strangulation, there can be no doubt of that, but she had a nasty bump on her head—occipital region. It must have been a fairly heavy blow. She's got a good mop of hair but it wasn't enough to cushion the impact much.'

'But it didn't kill her—the blow, I mean?'

'No, in my opinion the blow knocked her unconscious and then she was strangled.'

'How?'

'From the marks on her neck I should say by a nylon cord.'

Wycliffe nodded. 'Try this: she was making tea and while she was stooping to get a jug of milk from the refrigerator her assailant struck her across the base of the skull and she collapsed on the floor, he then strangled her with a nylon cord.'

Franks agreed. 'That would fit. Now, as to the time of death, I'll try to do better after the autopsy but at the moment I can't get closer than a few days.'

'As far as we know she was last seen alive exactly a week ago.'

'I wouldn't quarrel with that.' Franks took his coat from a chair and put it on. 'Well, I'm off. Get her over to me as quickly as you can and I'll let you have my report in the morning.'

The specialist at work, clear thinking, incisive. No bumbling there. Wycliffe envied him. He turned to find D.C. Dixon standing at his elbow and spoke brusquely, 'Nothing to do, Dixon? Do you know the Golden Cockerel?'

'Night club in Judson Street, sir. Limited gaming licence. Everybody calls it the Cock.'

'Indeed.' He was always a little moved as well as irritated by Dixon's anxiety to do and say the right thing. 'Well, the proprietor is a Maltese called Bourg. I want you to get hold of him and find out what you can about the girl. I think he lives in Palmerston Crescent.'

'I know the place, sir. A great Victorian barracks with about twenty rooms. He lives there with momma and eight kids. At least it was eight at the last count. They say he's devoted to them. Apparently his wife was a real doll when he married her, now she's as broad as she's long.'

'Really.'

Even Dixon was doing it.

'Just remember one thing, Dixon, Riccy Bourg may be the ideal husband and father but he's also a crook and a clever one so don't let him put anything over.'

'You can rely on me, sir.'

'I hope so. And Dixon—ask him what happened to his pianist?'

'Sir?'

Wycliffe explained.

Dixon went out and Wycliffe watched him go with a twinge of regret. When a case was on he wanted to be everywhere and to do everything; everything but what he was expected to do, to sit in his office and issue instructions.

'Have you been in the bedroom, sir?' Scales was going through the drawers of a built-in unit in the living room.

39

'Just glanced in, why?'

'She has a man who sleeps there pretty regularly.'

'I saw the dressing gown and slippers.'

Scales nodded. 'The bed linen too. She wasn't fussy about her laundry.'

Who had shared Debbie's bed? Surely not the tall, elegant gentleman Mrs Clarke had described; yet it would be surprising if Debbie had had a lover of whom her neighbour knew nothing.

'John!'

'Sir?'

'Get on to the ground landlords and find out who holds the lease on the flat and who pays the overheads.'

'I already have. The flat is in the girl's name and she paid all the bills herself.'

'Does this place have a back entrance?'

'And a service lift, sir. I told them to bring the mortuary van round the back; they're due any minute.'

Wycliffe decided that he might really be more use in his office. He went down in the lift without seeing a soul. Outside it was still raining and people were on their way home from work, the evening rush hour was beginning. Despite the rain a small crowd had gathered on the pavement though there was nothing to see but the fluted glass of the swing doors to the foyer. A reporter from the *News* accosted Wycliffe as he was getting into his car.

'Is it true that a girl has been murdered, Mr Wycliffe?'

'Quite true.' He was never needlessly coy with the press.

'Who was she?'

'A Miss Debbie Joyce; she was a singer at the Golden Cockerel. She was strangled.'

'When did it happen?'

'Her body was discovered this afternoon but she has been dead for several days.'

'Have you—?'

'I've told you all I know at the moment and I've got work to do.'

'Your man won't let me into the building.'

'There would be no point.'

# CHAPTER TWO

Wycliffe's headquarters occupied the first floor of one
wing of the new area police building. For almost a
fortnight it had been a lifeless place. People arrived at
nine in the morning and by five-fifteen most of the
offices were in darkness. His staff went about with an
air of listlessness as though what they were doing
might just as well have been left until the next day or
not done at all. It was, presumably, the same malaise
which had led him to stand by his big window,
watching the traffic and to murmur:

'Futile!'

But when he returned there at a little before six the
change was dramatic. Lights were on everywhere,
typewriters were clacking, telephones ringing and
people were bustling around with a new sense of
urgency and purpose. It was odd, because as yet very
few of them were involved in any way with the new
case. Even undertakers must get depressed when
business is slack.

He had scarcely sat at his desk when W.P.C. Saxton,
his clerical assistant, came in with a tray of tea.

'I thought you might be glad of that, sir.'

'Thank you, Diane.'

She was blonde, immaculate, always band-box fresh
and very efficient, like a secretary in a TV commercial.

She worried him: when she was near him he could not help wondering whether his collar was clean or if he had dandruff. He could not recall in what circumstances he had ever had the temerity to start calling her by her first name.

Reports were beginning to come in. First from D.C. Fowler who had questioned the caretaker and the occupants of the other flats. There were thirty-two flats in the building and he had spoken to someone in twenty-four of them. Only one person admitted to knowing anything about Debbie Joyce, a woman doctor on the seventh floor. Like most doctors she was prickly but Fowler was an old hand.

'Yes, I know the girl, at least I know of her.'

Fowler adopted a confidential manner and outlined what had happened in the flat below.

'Well, if, as you tell me, the girl is dead, I suppose there is no reason why I shouldn't tell you what happened. It was about three months ago, early October, between five and six in the morning, when I was awakened by someone ringing my doorbell. When I went to the door I found a young man in a dressing gown; he was distraught, barely coherent, but I gathered that there was someone ill in 602 and I went down with him.

'I found a young woman lying on the floor by the bed. She was recovering from an epileptic fit. I did what was necessary and got her back to bed. By that time she had completely recovered and she told me that she had been an epileptic since childhood but that in recent years her attacks had become less frequent and she had, rightly, given up taking the drugs which had been prescribed. I suggested, a little tartly, that if she had taken her husband into her confidence she could have avoided scaring him out of his wits. Of course, it emerged that the young man was not her husband.

'Anyway, I advised the girl to see her own doctor and

43

left them to it. As far as I was concerned that was the end of the matter.'

'Could you describe the young man or would you recognise him again if you saw him?'

'I can describe him and I have seen him again.'

'When have you seen him?'

'Two or three times, the last time was a fortnight ago. On each occasion we met in the lift, going up around midnight. To be honest I doubt whether I would have noticed him had he not been looking at me with a somewhat guilty expression which drew my attention. Then he spoke.'

The description was professionally detailed:

'Short—five feet five or six. Twentyish, slim with fair, curly hair and heavy sideburns; broad features, fresh complexion and rather cow-like brown eyes. On each occasion he wore blue jeans and a leather jacket with a checked shirt. Oh, yes, I remember, he had an old scar over his left eye. He struck me as a bit dim.'

'Do you practise from here?'

'No, I'm attached to a group practice at the Horton Health Centre.'

'Then how would he know that you are a doctor?'

'He may be dim but I imagine that he can read. My name is on the board in the hall—Dr Mary Peskett.'

Wycliffe was pleased; with that sort of description it shouldn't be difficult to pick up Debbie's sleeping partner. He was also interested to learn that she was an epileptic. Would this lead Franks to change his mind about the cause of her skull injury? In a grand mal attack the subject often threshes about with great violence; was it possible that she had come by her injury in this way? That the killer had then taken advantage of the fact that she was unconscious to finish her off? It sounded and was, almost certainly, absurd.

The truth was that Wycliffe had been troubled about the blow on the head. It was outside the usual pattern. Stranglers generally fall into one of two categories.

44

There are those who commit an unpremeditated crime in circumstances of unendurable frustration or anger and there are others who deliberately strangle out of perverted lust. For them the act of strangulation is associated with or is a substitute for the act of sex and they will go on killing until they are caught. In neither case is the victim likely to be knocked on the head first nor attacked while in the kitchen making tea.

D.C. Dixon was back from his interview with Bourg, the proprietor of the Golden Cockerel. He had been welcomed like an honoured guest and had been introduced to all the children from Marco aged two to Elisa who was sixteen.

'Momma, you hear this terrible thing? Little Debbie who sing at the club. Such a thing to happen.'

And Momma too was deeply distressed.

'She was a good girl,' Ricky went on. 'She work for me seven—no, eight months and everybody like her. She sing songs that are a little naughty but she look so ... what is the word? Pure? Chaste—that is it. All beautiful in a white dress like a little girl at her first communion in my village where I was born. People like that, men and women. They do not know whether to laugh a little or cry a little and that is good.'

He sighed. 'She was to do something special for when we open again on Wednesday. Tomorrow she would come for rehearsal.'

Mr Bourg absolutely refused to countenance the possibility that Debbie might have involved herself in anything discreditable. About the piano player he was contemptuous.

'He was a rogue that one. If Debbie set a little trap it was to help me; for proof of something I know already. In any case he was not good on the piano. That girl, she was as another daughter to me.'

After a pause for reflection he added: 'I tell you one thing and that is gossip only, you understand. It was said that Debbie is married and that she leave her

45

husband. Who she marry I do not know but you will find out.'

Asked who passed on this gossip he professed, grandly, never to remember such details.

Another pause and Mr Bourg reached his great conclusion. 'You find that bastard, her husband, my friend, he is the one for sure. And tell Mr Wycliffe that Riccardo Bourg give you this tip for free—no strings.'

Poor Dixon had been swamped by magnanimity and Wycliffe was highly amused even by the edited version of the interview which reached him.

The pattern was growing more complex, the colours richer. Riccy Bourg, his club, his singer, his wronged piano player and Debbie's illicit lover. Now there was the suggestion of a husband in the background.

Scales came in to say that, so far, he had been unable to trace Debbie's relatives; there had been almost nothing of a strictly personal nature in the flat. There was a cheque book but few of the counterfoils had been filled in.

'In the morning you can have a word with her bank manager.'

The wheels were beginning to turn. The description of the young man was being circulated to every policeman in the city; the occupants of the flats in Grenville House were being questioned for the second time, partly because husbands would be home, partly because they could now be questioned about the young man.

'I suppose we should get out an identikit picture of him?'

Wycliffe shrugged. 'If we don't pull him in tonight we can try it.'

He gave instructions for a man to remain in the flat through the night. 'As she was expected back today he might turn up.'

'Unless he killed her.'

\*    \*    \*

'There you are, Mr Norman.' His secretary helped him on with his overcoat, straightened his collar at the back and handed him his briefcase and gloves.

Norman glanced briefly round his office. 'You'll see that those files go back to registry, Miss Hopkins?'

'Right away, sir.'

He lingered in the doorway. 'They shouldn't be left here overnight.' A brief pause. 'Very well, nine-thirty in the morning.'

'Nine-thirty, Mr Norman. Good-night.'

Norman set off down the long corridor to the lift. He had to pass his surgical wards. The door of the television lounge was open and he could see several patients sitting round the set. The voice of a news reader reached him:

' . . . identified as Miss Debbie Joyce, a singer in one of the city's clubs. Detective Chief Superintendent Wycliffe stated that the police are treating her death as a case of murder.'

A domestic, pushing a trolley, steered round him and looked back with curiosity. A ward sister stopped, 'Are you all right, Mr Norman?'

He looked at her sharply. 'All right? Of course I'm all right.'

He walked on to the lift. A staff nurse, already in the lift on her way down, made herself as inconspicuous as possible. On the ground floor he stepped out of the lift and crossed the vast entrance hall. The porter dashed to open one of the doors.

'Good-night, Mr Norman, sir.'

It was raining, a fine drizzle, but his car was drawn up under the canopy. A middle-aged man in a chauffeur's cap opened the car door for him.

'A nasty night, sir.'

Norman sank into the back seat and said nothing.

The telephone rang.

'Wycliffe.'

'A Mr Matthew Norman on the line for you, sir, senior consultant surgeon at Millfield General.'

'Put him through.'

A cultured voice, dry and tight. 'I understand that a Miss Debbie Joyce has been murdered.'

'That is so.'

A moment of silence, then, 'I must talk to you, perhaps I could come to your office . . . '

'I would prefer to call on you.'

'As you wish. I live at twenty-four Conniston Gardens. What I have to tell you is important so the sooner you are able to come . . . '

'I'll be with you in half an hour.'


In the bottom flat at 14 Edgcumbe Close, Elaine Bennett was studying herself in the dressing table mirror. She was flushed, and she was feeling unwell. All day she had been conscious of a constriction in her throat, now it was painful and she had a headache.

Elaine was a nurse in private practice and her present job was nightnurse to a wealthy old lady who lived at Kemsley Rise, a bus trip across the city. For the past three weeks, each night, she had left the flat at half-past nine and walked to Godolphin Road where she boarded a 622 bus which took her to the bottom of Kemsley Rise. She had no day off for she preferred to work for short, intensive spells then take a week or two off between jobs. Her present job was something of a sinecure for she could sleep most of the night.

'I think I've got a temperature, Val.'

Valerie Hughes, her flat mate, was in the sitting room watching television but the door between was open.

'I told you.'

Elaine came through from the bedroom with a thermometer in her mouth. After a while she took it out and read it.

'A hundred and one.'

'I told you.'

48

'Can't you think of anything else to say?'

'Well, you can't go to work tonight, that's for sure.'

'But the old girl depends on me. If it gets round that I don't turn up at my cases I'm sunk.'

'She won't thank you for giving her the 'flu.'

'I suppose not. I'd better go out to the phone and ring the woman who does days. She might be willing to stop on.'

'I'll do it.'

'What? Ring?'

'No, look after the old woman. I suppose she would put up with me for one night.'

'But you're on six-till-two.'

'Tomorrow's my day off.' Valerie was a nurse at Millfield General.

'You're an angel! I do feel pretty bloody.'

'You look it.'

'Listen!' Elaine's attention had been caught by the television. An announcer was reading the regional news.

'. . . The dead girl is Debbie Joyce, a night club entertainer. A police spokesman said that she had been dead for several days when her body was found in the kitchen of her flat. The police are treating her death as murder.'

'Well, I'm damned!'

Valerie looked at her friend. 'That's the girl you went to school with, isn't it?'

'No.'

'But I remember you saying that night you went to the Cock—'

Elaine was suddenly irritable. 'You don't remember me saying I went to school with her because I didn't but I did know her when we were at school. We met playing hockey and we were friendly for a time.'

'Didn't you say Joyce wasn't her real name?'

'Whatever she's called now, her name when I knew her was Rosaline Parkin.'

49

'I wonder how she got herself murdered?'

'I would imagine that's easy enough if you carry on like she did at that club.' Elaine switched off the television. 'Now, for God's sake let's forget about it.'

Valerie shrugged. 'O.K. What are we going to eat?'

James Rendell locked the door of the shop, tried it twice, then stood on the edge of the pavement in the drizzling rain, waiting for a lull in the traffic down Prince's Street. It came and he crossed to a traffic island, waited again, then finally made it to the other side. It was not far to the city centre which was a blaze of light after the dark tunnel of Prince's Street. A man was selling newspapers in a shop doorway. A scrawled news-bill read: 'City Solicitor on Fraud Charge'. News of the discovery of Debbie Joyce's body had come too late for the evening editions.

Each working day for a week Rendell had forced himself to carry on normally, never leaving the shop between nine in the morning and half-past five in the afternoon. Each evening as he walked up Prince's Street to the city centre, he steeled himself for the moment when he would come in sight of the news-vendor and be able to read the legend on the news-bill. He would deliberately avert his eyes until he was within a couple of yards, then . . .

He could think of no circumstances in which the body could have remained undiscovered for a whole week. He told himself again and again that she was dead, there could be no doubt of that, no possible doubt. He had seen . . . but he would not think about what he had seen.

On the Wednesday evening, two days after, he had gone to the Golden Cockerel with no clear object in mind. He had certainly not intended to go in but it came as a shock when from the end of Judson Street, he saw that the club was in darkness, the sign unlit. He hurried down the street, his heart thumping wildly. There was

50

a little notice on one of the glass doors which he had difficulty in reading because of the dim light. By bringing his eyes close to the square of cardboard he could make out the words: 'The Management regrets that the club will remain closed for ten days during which time the premises will be redecorated and modernised to give patrons a better service in the future.'

For a while he was almost prepared to believe that this was part of a plan to deceive him, to lead him to some incriminating act. Was it possible that the police, for their own reasons, would hush up the fact that a crime had been committed? The thought scared him although he would not have been able to explain why.

Later that same evening he had gone to a side street from which it was possible to see the upper floors of Grenville House and for more than an hour he had stood there watching the windows which he knew belonged to her flat. They were in total darkness. On the Friday in desperation he had almost telephoned the police to lay anonymous information.

The weekend had been purgatory. How could he go on without knowing what was happening? Now it was Monday again. A whole week.

'Goodnight, guv.' The old man with the newspapers had got to know him although he never bought a paper.

He walked on. It was not far to the *Guardian* building where he lived with his sister and brother-in-law. The couple had a flat on the top floor of the office block of which they were caretakers. He took the lift and came out into a tiny vestibule on the eighth floor.

'Is that you, Jim?'

He went into his bedroom, washed, and changed his jacket for a woolly cardigan then he went through into the living room where they would soon be sitting down to their evening meal. His sister, Alice, was in the kitchen but he could talk to her through the open hatch.

'Where's Albert?'

'They got trouble with the radiators on the third. He's down there with the maintenance man. He said not to wait. Had a good day?'

'All right.'

'You don't look very well, Jim, and that's a fact.'

'I'm all right.'

He had been a fool to come to live with his sister and her husband; it would have been better if he had stayed on in his own house, alone. Now he had to keep up this constant pretence and, worse, endure their sympathy and professed understanding when they understood nothing—nothing!

The television was on as usual. The regional news. '. . . Debbie Joyce, a night club entertainer. A police spokesman said that she had been dead several days when her body was found in the kitchen of her flat. The police are treating her death as murder.'

He had been waiting so long, yet now that it had come it was like an unexpected blow. His legs would not support him and he sat down heavily.

'What was that, Jim—about a girl being murdered?'

He did not answer, he could not trust his voice.

'Weren't you listening?'

'What?'

Alice was irritated. 'It doesn't matter, forget it.'

He was recovering and experiencing a great flood of relief. His spirits rose, he began to feel almost gay.

By the time Alice had served the meal he was so excited that he could scarcely eat his food. She noticed the change in him and, as usual, misinterpreted the signs.

'What you need is a complete change, Jim. Why don't you take a few days off—go up to London and poke around the museums and art galleries? You used to love doing that.'

'I don't need a change, I'm perfectly all right.' He spoke between his teeth, he was so irritated by her chatter. Why couldn't she shut up and leave him alone?

'Old Probert would keep the shop going—do him good, he'd miss you.'

'I said I'm all right, Alice. For God's sake stop telling me what to do!'

It was so unusual for him to raise his voice that Alice was upset.

'There's no need to rave at me, Jim. I'm only trying to help you. You want me to mind my own business, all right, I will.'

'I'm sorry.' He realised that he had gone too far. 'Really.'

But he was trembling and as soon as he could he left the table.

'Are you going out?'

'I thought I would.'

He went into his bedroom and put on his mackintosh and cap. He felt in the right-hand pocket of his mackintosh and was reassured. His nerves became steadier and his hands ceased to tremble. Before leaving he looked in the living room.

'You mustn't mind me, Alice, it's very good of you and Albert to have me here. Maybe you're right, perhaps I will have a few days but I'll wait for the better weather.'

\*      \*      \*

Wycliffe telephoned Franks but the pathologist was unimpressed by the news that Debbie Joyce had been epileptic.

'Anything else? Otherwise I'll get on . . . '

Wycliffe was unusually diffident. 'Not about the girl, at least, not directly. I wanted to ask you, do you know Matthew Norman, the senior surgeon at Millfield?'

'As we work almost under the same roof, I'd have a job not to.'

53

'What sort of man is he?'

Even close friendship fails to compete with the Masonic solidarity of the medical profession. 'He's a good surgeon, one of the best.'

'I don't doubt it, but what sort of man is he?'

'Rather severe. He sets high standards for himself and for the people who work with him. He sometimes appears patronising but I don't think that he means to be so.'

'Married?'

Wycliffe could sense the pathologist's hesitation.

'I understand that he is separated from his wife though I know very little of his private life.'

'Any gossip about women?'

'Definitely not!' It was amusing to hear the emphatic almost shocked denial from Franks whose own affairs were notorious.

'Or the other thing?'

'Nor that.'

'All right, thanks.'

But now Franks' curiosity was aroused. 'Is he supposed to be mixed up in this affair?'

'That's what I'm going to ask him.'

'Be careful. He comes from a legal family, his father was Recorder of the city and his grandfather was a high court judge.'

'I'll remember.'

It was Franks who was now reluctant to end the conversation. 'From what I've heard, he lives for his work and his pots.'

'His pots?'

'Chinese blue-and-white porcelain. He's an authority.'

Wycliffe put down the receiver with a smile on his face.

Conniston Gardens was a crescent of large, Edwardian houses on the edge of Conniston Park. Giant elms, now bare, gave the place an air of slightly decaying elegance and it would have been no surprise to hear the clip-clop of horse's hooves as the brougham drew up, bringing the master from the station.

Wycliffe was received by the housekeeper and taken to a back room where Norman waited. He was very tall, slim but slightly pot-bellied. His head was abnormally large but his features were small and close together, a ready-made caricature. No need to look further for Debbie's well-dressed visitor.

'Good of you to come, chief superintendent. Sherry?'

There were enough books to call the room a library; the bookshelves reached to within a yard of the high ceiling and blue-and-white vases and jars were disposed along the tops of the bookcases. Glass-fronted cabinets on either side of the chimney breast housed smaller pieces. A large gas fire burned cosily in a fireplace framed by a huge white-marble mantelpiece. Above the fireplace there was a portrait in oils of a man in legal gown and wig. A severe, distinguished face whose features resembled Norman's but were more fittingly proportioned and disposed.

Wycliffe watched the surgeon with bland, expressionless eyes. Norman was finding it difficult to begin, he was the sort of man who would abhor any discussion of his intimate life.

'I heard on the television news that a young woman by the name of Joyce had been found dead in her flat. It was said that she had been murdered.'

'That is so.'

'I hoped that you would be prepared to give me more information.'

Wycliffe was cool. 'If I am satisfied that you are entitled to it.'

'She was my wife.'

'I see.'

Norman had got over the first hurdle and his manner became noticeably less tense. 'We were married a year ago but we separated after three months.'

'How long since you last saw your wife, Mr Norman?'

'A little over a week.'

'You visited her regularly?'

'Fairly regularly?'

'Why?'

A flicker of annoyance. 'She was my wife, the fact that we were separated did not mean that I was indifferent to her welfare.'

'Or she to yours?'

He ignored the question.

Wycliffe's manner was brusque, almost rude. Norman moved in a world where his word was law. Doctors, nurses and patients, patients in particular, held him almost in reverence. Daily, life and death lay, literally, in his hands. In those circumstances a man is bound to develop an armour of self esteem. To get him to talk freely about himself it was essential to break through.

'You have always lived in this house?'

'I was born here, my father was Recorder of the city.' He glanced up at the portrait over the mantelpiece.

'You live alone?'

A mild show of well-bred irritation. 'My housekeeper and her husband have a flat upstairs.'

Wycliffe was trying to picture the dead girl in these surroundings, sharing them with this man. If, as her neighbour had suggested, she enjoyed hurting people she had a ready-made victim in her shy, sensitive husband.

'Why did you marry her?'

Norman's anger flared. 'I really do not see . . . '

'Your wife has been murdered and such questions will have to be answered.'

He pursed his lips and seemed to consider. 'I suppose that you are right. It would be foolish to hamper the investigations in any way.'

Thank God for the objectivity of a trained mind.

'You were a man in your late forties, a bachelor, living in the house where you were born—'

It was Norman's turn to interrupt. 'Because a man is a bachelor, it does not necessarily follow that he wishes to be so.'

'But a girl in her twenties with a totally alien background . . .'

Outside it was quite dark but the curtains had not been drawn. Norman stood up, went to the window and swept them together in a single vigorous movement.

'A man comes to terms with circumstances. Perhaps he solves his problems by pretending that they do not exist then something happens and pretence is no longer possible.'

Wycliffe looked instinctively at the shelves of books, the valuable porcelain, the desk and the well-worn swivel chair. His glance did not escape Norman who smiled, wryly.

'It wasn't enough.'

'How did you meet her?'

'By the most improbable chance. From time to time the staff at the hospital organise a dance and the consultants are expected to look in. A gesture. On this occasion Debbie was there, she had been invited by one of my juniors.' He broke off. 'Perhaps I should tell you that although she insisted on being called Debbie, it was not her real name. She was Rosaline Parkin, and she adopted the name Debbie Joyce for professional reasons. Anyway, she was there and it happened that I was standing by the buffet when she was choosing what she would have. She made it her business to draw me into conversation. At first I was a little distant but before long I found myself talking freely. Someone had told her of my interest in Chinese blue-and-white and she asked me several intelligent questions. It was clear that she knew nothing about the subject but her interest seemed genuine. To my own astonishment I found

57

myself asking her to come and see my collections.' He gestured helplessly. 'She came and we went on from there.'

The sound of a table being laid came from an adjoining room, the rattle of crockery and cutlery.

Wycliffe was asking himself whether the interview could have gone quite in this way if Norman had murdered his wife. He had to admit that he had no data to go on. The Normans of this world are not often involved with the police and so in dealing with them there are few precedents.

But the surgeon's manner had changed. He was much more relaxed. Wycliffe suspected that this introspective and essentially solitary man was finding a certain relief in unburdening himself in a strictly professional context.

'For the first time in my life I fell in love. The phrase is an apt one, it precisely describes what happened to me — I fell, as helpless to control or influence my fate as a man who steps off a cliff.' He paused. 'It was a devastating experience. Do you find that absurd, superintendent?'

'If I found human nature absurd I should not be doing this job.'

Norman looked at him appreciatively. 'No, I suppose not; nor I mine.'

He pointed to the decanter. 'Are you sure that you won't?'

'Very well, thank you.'

They were silent while he poured the sherry with that economy of movement and precision which is only found in people who daily rely on the skill of their hands.'

'Somebody said that a fool at forty must be a fool indeed. Of course, I asked her to marry me and she agreed. I did not question my fortune any more than one questions waking on a spring morning. Little things might have warned me but I was in no mood to be warned. We were married.'

A long pause during which he sipped his sherry and stared at the fire.

'It was like having a chair snatched from under you when you are about to sit down. Overnight she seemed to become a different person. You asked me why I married her, the question for me is, why did she marry me? I asked myself that question many times during each day and night that we were together and I still do not know the answer. It is true that I am comfortably off but she was not interested in my money. I have some status but she did not care about that either. She married me yet she seemed to have hated me—why?'

'Why, indeed?

'When she left me my first feeling was one of relief.' He gestured weakly with his long, white hands. 'But you cannot live with a girl like her, even as we lived, without missing her when she goes.'

'You tried to persuade her to come back?'

He nodded without speaking.

Wycliffe looked up at the Recorder's portrait and wondered what genetic cookery had produced this chancy blend of sophistication and naivety, of priggishness and sensuality, of pedantry and quirkish humour.

'Did you visit your wife last Monday?'

'Last Monday? Is that when . . . '

Wycliffe said nothing.

'No, I did not see her on Monday, I was at the hospital all day, at least, until half-past six or seven in the evening.'

'Just one more thing. Can you tell me anything of her background, her relatives, where she went to school and who her friends were?'

Norman shook his head. 'I must confess that I knew very little about her and the fact worried me. One's wife . . . But she was secretive. She told me once that she had lost her parents when she was a baby and that she had been brought up by a maiden aunt. That was all.'

'Did she leave any of her personal things here—letters, documents, that sort of thing?'

'She took everything with her, not that she had much. When she left her belongings went into two suitcases.' He looked at Wycliffe then at his room, stored with possessions. 'That moved me deeply.'

'Is that why you set her up in the flat and paid her bills?'

Resentment flickered again then died. He nodded. 'I made her an allowance and I bought the flat in her name. It was the least I could do.'

Another silence, so profound that they could hear the faint hissing of the gas fire.

'How did she die?'

'She was strangled after being knocked unconscious by a blow to the head.'

'Have you any idea who might have killed her?'

'None.'

'The club where she worked has an unsavoury reputation.'

'All the possibilities are being investigated.'

'Of course.' Norman came with him to the gate. 'Thank you for coming.'

'You realise that you may be the subject of further investigation?'

'Yes.'

The rain had almost stopped and a pale radiance in the sky betrayed the position of the moon above the clouds.

He drove home slowly. The move which had cost him his office in a Queen Anne crescent had enabled him to become the proud owner of the Watch House, an old coastguard house built on the slopes overlooking the narrows through which all the shipping entering and leaving the port had to pass. A half acre of ground went with the house and, altogether, it was a great consolation to him on days when he threatened himself with an early retirement.

Ever since their marriage their home had been a place where he could relax. He took it for granted, scarcely realising that it was a rare talent of his wife's which made it so. In more than twenty years, even through the twins' most difficult periods, there had been few crises and none which threatened their marriage.

'Back to normal?'

'A girl strangled in one of the new flats in the city centre.'

'Is Jimmy Gill back?'

'No, but he will be as soon as he hears about this.'

He bathed, had his meal, helped to wash up then they sat together in front of the fire, reading and listening to records.

At nine o'clock he switched on the television for the news. The finding of Debbie Joyce's body was mentioned again. 'The police are treating it as a case of murder.'

Just after ten the telephone rang. It was Gill.

'I'm at the office. I heard about the girl so I looked in to see what was going on. I'd no sooner arrived than another report came through, an attack on a girl in the Godolphin Road area. She's been taken to Millfield. I gather that she made the 999 call herself so she can't be all that bad but I thought you'd better know.'

# CHAPTER THREE

Valerie came back into the sitting room dressed for the street. 'Three aspirins, a glass of hot milk and bed for you. And don't forget to use disinfectant when you wash up.'

Elaine smiled weakly. 'Thanks, Val.'

Valerie opened the street door and banged it shut behind her. The air was moist and chilly but the rain had stopped. A thin mist drifted tenuously between the houses and haloed the street lamps. She hurried up the Close to a point where a convenient footpath cut through to Godolphin Road saving a quarter of a mile of walking. It led through allotments between ragged privet hedges. As she turned into the path it started to rain again, sweeping across the open ground. She was not a nervous girl but she did not care for this walk at night. The street lamps in Godolphin Road seemed a long way off. But who would be out on a night like this unless they had to be? She focused her thoughts on the winter coat she had bought in the sales and plodded on through the darkness.

She was half way through the allotments when a sudden movement, very close, startled her. She did not cry out and when she would have done it was too late, all she could manage was a choking gurgle. Her face was pressed hard against the material of a man's raincoat and there was something round her neck which made it almost impossible to breathe. She knew that he was trying to strangle her but she could not really believe it. The cord, or whatever it was, cut into the back of her neck but in front her coat collar had caught in it. All the same ... She struggled and her waterproof hat fell off. Her head felt as though it would burst but she had not lost consciousness. Then the pressure was suddenly released and a man's voice said, 'Oh, God! Oh, God!' He moved away from her and she slipped to the ground in a sitting position, her head fell back into the privet bush and the twigs scratched her face and ears. She heard the man pounding off in the direction of the Close.

The odd thing was that she did not feel very frightened but she could not muster the strength to shout or move. After a little while she was able to drag herself to her feet. She had been sitting in mud which stuck to her clothing and she muttered to herself, 'Christ, I'm in a mess.' The thing was to get to a telephone.

She could not bring herself to go in the direction which her attacker had gone so she made for Godolphin Road. She remembered that there was a call-box where the footpath joined the main road. She felt weak and sick and giddy and her throat was painful but she made it. Godolphin Road was utterly deserted and she had difficulty in opening the door of the call-box but she got inside, lifted the receiver and dialled 999.

'Which service do you require?' The voice, cool and detached.

'Police.'

She managed to answer their questions then collapsed on the floor of the box leaving the receiver dangling on its cord. She did not lose consciousness, only the ability to move. She heard the police car arrive and she was afraid they would not see her but she could not call or get up. However there was no need; a constable bent over her and a little later she heard the ambulance.

In the end they put her to bed in the accident ward of her own hospital. She sat up, not displeased with the attention she was getting and rather glad that the scratches on her face and neck and the bruises on her throat made her look worse than she felt. But she was enough of a nurse to know that it would be a different story in the morning.

A plain-clothes policeman came in and sat by her bed. A nurse drew the curtains round her bed to give some privacy. The policeman told her that he was Detective Superintendent Wycliffe but he looked an amiable and kindly man.

'What about telling your parents where you are?'

She was not a local girl, her parents lived in Bristol and she said that the ward sister had arranged for them to be told.

'Now, if it doesn't upset you too much I want you to tell me what happened in as much detail as you can remember.'

She did so and her story was coherent and told with remarkable self-possession.

'That's fine, now two or three questions and I'll leave you in peace.' He smiled encouragement. 'Did you see his face? . . . Was he much taller than you? . . . You say that you had your face pressed against his coat . . . '

She tried to explain that, in fact, she had seen nothing. The man must have been a good deal taller than she was but that meant little for she was only five feet two.

'You said just now that your hat fell off.'

'Oh, yes it did. My waterproof hat, a sort of sou'-wester.'

'I know, one of our chaps picked it up. Was it immediately after your hat fell off that he let you go?'

She considered, her forehead wrinkled under blonde hair. 'Yes, I think it was—it must have been.'

'He let you go, you slipped to the ground and you heard him say, "Oh, God!"—twice, then he ran off. Is that it?'

'Yes.'

Wycliffe wished that he might smoke. 'I would like you to think about my next question very carefully before you answer. Did you get any impression—any impression at all—as to why he released you?'

Again the puzzled frown. 'I've thought about it, of course.'

'It wasn't that you succeeded in breaking free from him?'

'Oh, no, he could have done it if he'd wanted to.' She shuddered without affectation. 'I can't say for certain but it seemed to me that he could have been shocked and frightened by what he was doing. Does that sound silly?'

'Not a bit! You mean that he could have been someone subject to fits of violence and that, fortunately, he came out of this particular fit and was horrified by what he found himself doing?'

'Yes, does it seem likely?'

Wycliffe did not say but he thought not. Certainly there are psychopathic killers who appear to be quite normal and to have little or no recollection of their crimes between attacks, but Dr Jekyll does not supplant Mr Hyde in the act.

'You don't think that he mistook you for someone else and that when your hat fell off he realised his mistake?'

He saw from her expression that he had hit the mark.

'It was Elaine he was after! He must have stopped when my hat fell off because he saw my fair hair— Elaine is dark.'

'Elaine?'

'The girl I share a flat with. She should have been going through the allotments at that time, not me.' She explained.

'I'll be back.' He pushed through the curtain and looked up and down the ward for the sister. He met her in the passage and she must have been impressed by his gravity of manner for when he snapped, 'Telephone!' she led him to her office without a word and left.

He was put through to headquarters and to Gill. 'This attack, Jimmy, it looks as though he went for the wrong girl, he was after her flat mate, Elaine Bennett . . . '

'They've just found her.'

'Found her?'

'I sent a crime car to Edgcumbe Close to break the news—to tell this Bennett girl that her pal was in hospital. Constable Allen couldn't get any answer although there were lights on in the flat. When he pushed the door he found that it was unlatched and there she was, lying in the hall, strangled.'

'How long since?'

'Allen's message was timed at 22.31. I got the circus on the road and I was just going to phone you when your call came through.'

'Are you going there?'

'I'm on my way.'

Wycliffe was shaken. The cold resolution behind the killing dismayed him. A mistake, rectified as soon as possible. Logic. But what logic!

He went back to the ward, his every move watched by the other patients.

'I've just thought of something else,' Valerie said. 'A funny smell . . . it was when my face was against his raincoat.'

'What sort of smell?'

It was not the first time he had faced the problem of getting a witness to describe a smell. What an opportunity for some ingenious boffin to contrive an odour identikit!

'It could have been paint or varnish, or even the polish they sometimes use on floors.'

'You mean wax polish?'

'Yes, I suppose I do.'

A moment of silence while she looked at him with worried eyes.

'Why did he want to kill Elaine?'

'I don't know.'

'Have you told her?'

'One of our cars called round some time ago.'

'She would have been in bed. You know she's got the 'flu?'

'You told me.'

Before leaving the hospital he talked with the sister. Under her professional gloss she seemed perturbed. 'No, I agree, it would be most unwise to tell her tonight; she's had enough, poor girl!' But Wycliffe had the impression that her thoughts were elsewhere. In the end it came. 'I think that I have probably been foolish . . .'

He waited.

'A few minutes ago a man telephoned to enquire after Valerie. He knew her name, he spoke of her as "Valerie Hughes, the girl who was attacked on the allotments".'

'What did he want?'

'Just to know how she was, he seemed concerned.'

It might be significant. Valerie had dragged herself to a call-box in Godolphin Road and dialled 999. A patrol car and ambulance had been sent but there had been few people about to see. Not many could know of the attack even now and who would know the identity of the girl?

'You told him she was in no danger?'

'I am afraid I did.'

'What was his reaction?'

'He seemed relieved.'

'The call came through the switchboard?'

'Of course!'

The switchboard operator remembered the call. 'He wanted to know if the girl who had been attacked on the allotments had been admitted. He sounded genuinely

67

worried and I saw no harm in putting him through to the ward sister.'

'Call-box or private subscriber?'

The operator reflected. 'Private, I'm sure of that. I mean, I didn't have to wait for the call-box routine.'

'Can you place the time of the call?'

'It was a few minutes after eleven.'

The girl's 999 call had been logged at 21.43 which meant that the attack had probably taken place at 21.30 or thereabout. If the call to the hospital had been made from the man's home—and from where else could such a call have been made?—it meant that he had gone to the house in Edgcumbe Close, committed the second crime and reached home in an hour and a half. Not much to go on, especially as there was nothing to show whether he had a car, used public transport or merely walked. But that was the kind of evidence the police were good at getting. Even on a dark, misty night it was unlikely that he could have moved about much without being seen by somebody. There was a chance.

He was inclined to believe that the call to the hospital had come from the killer and that it was made out of concern for the girl he had mistakenly attacked. But other interpretations were possible and to guard against a second attack on Valerie Hughes he arranged for a round-the-clock police guard at the hospital.

Edgcumbe Close was near the hospital, a quiet cul-de-sac of small, detached villas, several of them converted into flats to attract hospital staff. Number fourteen had been properly converted with separate access to the top flat by an outside staircase at the back. The close was crowded with police vehicles, a van which looked like a black maria, waiting for the body, a Range Rover and three patrol cars. A uniformed policeman at the gate saluted Wycliffe. The mist was turning to rain again.

'They're using the window, sir.'

To avoid the hall where the body was, Wycliffe

climbed in. The front room seemed to be full of men and he could hear Smith, the photographer, cursing the hall. 'Not enough bloody room to stand sideways . . . you need a sodding skyhook in this place!'

Franks was there and came over to Wycliffe. 'We seem to be back in business with a vengeance. Not much I can tell you. She was strangled, no doubt of that, but no blow to the head this time. Death occurred between, say half-past nine and ten. I arrived here about five minutes to eleven.'

Wycliffe nodded and turned to Scales who looked pale and weary. 'Go home, get some rest. Where's Mr Gill?'

'Mr Gill is upstairs talking to the girls in the upper flat. They are both nurses and they were on the two-till-ten shift. They arrived home about twenty minutes past ten but there's a separate entrance to their flat and they had no idea that anything was amiss.'

Smith was packing up his photographic gear. Wycliffe went out into the hall. Elaine's body was lying where it had fallen, one leg doubled under her, her back against the wall. She was wearing a green dressing gown over a baby-doll nightie. She must have been going to bed or already in bed when her murderer arrived. From where he stood the mop of black curls almost covered her face. Despite his years in the force he always found it hard to come to terms with violent death, especially of the young and this was the second body he had seen in a single day.

Gill's voice came through from the front room and Wycliffe went to join him.

'Nobody seems to have heard a thing. There was nobody upstairs when it happened and the neighbours are blind and deaf. These bloody suburbs, nobody cares a fart whether you live or die.' Gill too, was moved by the senseless killing.

Wycliffe went through into the room behind the sitting room to which there was a communicating door.

A bedroom with twin beds. Bright and chintzy but almost squalid in its untidiness. Powder spilled on the carpet, clothes all over the place. One of the beds had the clothes thrown back. There was a second door into a bathroom and loo for midgets. He had to go out into the hall again to reach the kitchen which had the things kitchens usually have and a sink-full of dirty dishes. What is it which turns bachelor girls into house-proud mums?

The front door was open, rain blew into the hall. They were moving the body.

'There's nothing for us here.'

'Nothing.'

James Rendell sat on the stairs in the front hall of the suburban house. The front door and the door leading into the sitting room were both shut and there was just room for a hall-stand and a telephone table. The hall lantern was fitted with ruby glass but the man's features were grey, scarcely warmed by the reddish glow. He wore a wet mackintosh and he held his hands tightly clasped between his knees to stop them trembling. For a long time he had been staring at the black and white tiles on the floor which seemed to change their pattern as he watched, then when it seemed, at last, that he was sufficiently composed he reached for the telephone and dialled a number. He listened while the instrument went through its repertoire of click and burrs.

'Millfield Hospital.'

He made a tremendous effort to keep his voice steady. 'I wanted to enquire about Valerie Hughes—the girl who was attacked on the allotments.'

'Hold on, please.'

An interval of silence than a woman's voice. 'Ward sister speaking. Are you a relative?'

He hesitated. 'A friend—a friend of the family.'

'Miss Hughes is suffering from shock.'

70

'She'll be all right?'

Oh, yes. She needs rest and quiet.'

'Thanks—thank you.'

'Who shall I say—'

He dropped the receiver. He was shivering now, his hands once more clasped between his knees, his body doubled up, contracted as though he would shrink into himself.

The minutes passed. A car stopped nearby, he heard voices, doors slamming then silence once more. He was becoming calmer but the dampness seemed to be seeping through to his bones.

He reached for the telephone again and dialled.

'474655.' A woman's voice.

He did not answer at once for, suddenly, his voice had let him down. The number was repeated on a rising note of impatience.

'Is that you, Alice?'

'Who'd you think it is, the Queen of Sheba?'

'It's Jim.'

'You don't say!'

'I think I'll stay here for the night, I don't feel like coming back just now.'

The woman sighed. 'You're being silly, Jim. What good can it do? You'll just brood over there on your own and make yourself worse. The last bus hasn't gone yet, you could still make it . . .'

'No, I think I'll stay, just for tonight.'

'All right, if you must. Make sure you have a hot drink before you go to bed. And what about breakfast? Have you got any eggs?'

'I've got everything I need thanks.'

'Well, all right. What else can I say?'

'Nothing. See you tomorrow evening after work.'

'Yes. All right. Good-night Jim.'

'Good-night, Alice.'

'And Jim . . .'

'What is it?'

71

'You won't do anything silly, will you?'

'Of course not.'

Wycliffe drove slowly through the wet, all but deserted streets, to his headquarters.

In the darkened building the C.I.D. floor was a brilliant band of light. Wycliffe went through the duty room and up the stairs to his office. It was rarely that he used the lift. Another protest against something indefinable, part of his resentment of this crude, new, impersonal building in which he had to work; in which, perhaps, he saw some threat to his identity.

Gill joined him in his office.

'Elaine Bennett, twenty-five, free-lance nurse, at present nursing an old woman out at Kemsley Rise. She's been on that job for the past three weeks and each night she's taken the route through the allotments to pick up a bus in Godolphin Road. I got this from the girls upstairs. They also told me that her parents ran a bakery business in the city until a couple of years ago, now they've retired and they've got a little bungalow at Paignton.'

'Have they been told?'

'I passed it to the Paignton nick, they'll see to it.' He took out a cheroot and lit it, flicking the match on the carpet.

Wycliffe filled his pipe. Two girls murdered and a third attacked, apparently in error. A week separated the two killings. Were they linked? There was nothing to suggest it except the improbability that there were two killers loose in the city and the fact that both girls had been strangled.

'The girls upstairs also told me that Elaine had a boyfriend, a chap called Nigel something, they can't remember what but they think it's Sears or Swears. They don't know where he lives or where he works but they gave me a passable description and he's got a red Mini.

72

'They're naturally a bit coy about speaking their minds now but it's obvious they didn't like her. She was a staff nurse at Millfield and chucked up her job to go into private nursing. The girls obviously feel that the hospital wasn't good enough for her.'

The telephone rang.

'Wycliffe.'

It was D.C. Dixon. Wycliffe had forgotten all about him, spending the night in Debbie Joyce's flat.

'He walked in ten minutes ago, sir, opened the door with his own key.'

'Who walked in?'

'Debbie's boyfriend, sir, the man she's been sleeping with. He's with me now and he's had quite a shock.'

'I'll send a car, you can pack up at the flat and bring him in.'

No sooner had Wycliffe passed on the news to Gill than they were interrupted again, this time by the press and Wycliffe had to go out to give them a statement.

It was one o'clock when Dixon arrived with the young man who had been Debbie's sleeping partner. Wycliffe saw Dixon in his office, alone, before tackling him.

'He took it badly, sir. I'd say he'd had the shock of his life. He's called Frisby, Donald Frisby, and he's been spending most of his nights at the flat for the past four months. He's an assistant projectionist at the Ritz cinema and he shares a flat with three other chaps; a real bachelor pad if you ask me.'

All these young people belonged to the same age group as Dixon yet his attitude towards them was that of an older man, censorious and a little patronising. It was the policeman talking. Was he the same off duty?

'He knew that she should be back today?'

'Yes, sir. He says she told him that she would be in London for a week and that she would be back in the flat tonight.'

The doctor's description had been accurate. The

dark brown eyes and blond, curly hair were in striking contrast. His build was slight and there was something vaguely feminine about him. He wore the same clothes as the doctor had described: blue jeans, checked shirt and leather jacket. He looked pale and confused, no more than a boy.

Wycliffe had had tea sent up and offered him a cup. He drank it down greedily.

'I can't think why anybody wanted to kill her.' His lip was trembling.

'You know that she was married?'

'Married? Debbie? I can't believe that!'

'But it's true, I was talking to her husband earlier this evening. Her husband bought the flat and paid the expenses but they lived separately.'

The rather vacant face darkened. 'Was it him?'

Wycliffe answered obliquely. 'I don't think he knew of your existence.'

Frisby looked at the chief superintendent, his eyes troubled. 'I don't know what to say. She went to London to look for a job in one of the clubs. If she got one she was going to move up there and I was going to join her later on. We were going to set up together.'

'Where did you meet?'

'At a party, one Sunday. You know how it is, there was a swop round of partners and I found myself with Debbie. I don't usually get that sort of luck.'

'When was this party?'

He looked vague. 'I can't remember exactly. September some time, I think.'

'She gave you a key to her flat?'

'After a bit. You see, she works till two in the morning and I'm not through at the cinema till half-eleven so I took up to go round to the Cock to pick her up. The trouble with that was that it cost money; Riccy, that's her boss, don't like to see people just sitting, you got to be spending money one way or another. Anyway, Debbie said if I had a key I could go straight to the flat and that's what I've been doing.' He brought out a packet of cigarettes then thought better of it and put them away again.

'Smoke if you want to.'

'Thanks.'

'What time did you leave the flat each morning?'

'Between ten and eleven as a rule.'

'It's odd that Debbie's neighbour doesn't seem to know about you.'

He smiled, sheepishly. 'You mean the old dear in 604? Debbie made sure of that, she used to keep cavy for me every morning. Just out of devilment to keep the old so and so guessing, she said.'

'Do you know a girl called Elaine Bennett? She's a nurse.'

'Can't say I do. I don't know any nurses.'

'You didn't sleep at the flat while Debbie was away?'

'No, she wouldn't have liked that.'

'Why not?'

It was too much for him but he tried, 'Well, I know it sounds a bit odd, specially seeing she's ... what I'm trying to say is, she liked to run things. I mean, you had to remember ... '

'To remember what?'

He shifted uncomfortably in his chair. 'It's hard to say.'

'You had to remember that she was boss, is that it?'

'I suppose so.' He studied the end of his cigarette for a moment. 'She wasn't exactly bossy but she liked to set the pace, if you understand me.'

'How old are you. Twenty?'

'Nineteen.'

Wycliffe questioned him for the better part of an hour then let him go. He learned very little.

Poor sap. '"She liked to set the pace",' Wycliffe muttered, 'I'll bet she did. In every way.'

Donald Frisby, 19, Assistant Projectionist at the Ritz Cinema.

Matthew Norman, 48, Senior Consultant Surgeon at Millfield General.

An object lesson in the irony of sex but there was more to it than that.

A middle-aged man, inhibited and shy; a not very bright youngster of nineteen who could scarcely be regarded as a type specimen of male virility. Lady Bountiful distributes her largesse. The message was clear. No male chauvinist pigs need apply.

Wycliffe sat alone in his office with only the green-shaded desk lamp lighting the big room. It was utterly quiet, the world could have died around him.

When he heard of Elaine's death, while he was still at Valerie Hughes' bedside, his first reaction had been disbelief followed by dismay. It was the cold resolution of the killing which had dismayed him—like an execution.

The killer must have rung the doorbell more than once. Elaine had gone to bed and it would have taken her a while to get up, put on a dressing gown and answer the door. Meanwhile he had stood waiting in the rain. What had he said to her? He must have been intensely excited. Had he managed to disguise his feelings? At least sufficiently for her to admit him without creating a major scene on the doorstep. The fact that he had used Valerie's name in ringing the hospital meant that he knew the girls and probably the set-up at the flat.

'I wanted to let you know that Valerie has had an accident.'

'An accident? You'd better come in.'

And then in the little hall, she, totally unsuspecting . . .

No need of a preliminary blow to prevent a struggle or to stop her from screaming. Before she could scream it was too late.

And what about the other case? The murder of Debbie Joyce or Rosaline Norman née Parkin. Here too the killer had been admitted to the girl's flat. She was, it seemed, making him a cup of tea. Did this mean that she knew him? Not necessarily, but if not he must have told a convincing story. But here the circumstances were very different from the murderer's point of view. He was on the sixth floor of a large building with people coming and going all the time. There were probably people in the flats above and below and on the other side of the thin partitioning walls. There must be no struggle, no possibility that she would scream. At a suitable moment, when she was stooping getting milk from the refrigerator, he struck. Again, in the cold, calculating efficiency of the crime there was the suggestion of an execution.

Wycliffe smiled sourly. He had at least talked himself round to the conviction that both crimes were the work of the same hand.

He drove home through empty streets. The rain had stopped and it was turning colder. As he got clear of the city he could see the moon riding high through a rift in the clouds and when he turned off the road into his own, private lane the Watch House lay below him, white in the moon-light and the navigation lights in the estuary were pale and insignificant.

He undressed in the bathroom and posted himself between the sheets but Helen woke.

'What time is it?'

'Half-past two.'

'Sure you wouldn't like something?'

'Yes, six hours sleep.'

She kissed him lightly and turned over. Within minutes her regular breathing told him that she was asleep.

He was not so lucky. How long was it since he had stood by his window, watching the traffic and complaining of futility? Less than twelve hours. But during that time the body of a murdered girl had been discovered, another girl had been brutally attacked and a third had been murdered. During that time ... as often when he tried to reconstruct events in a coherent and orderly fashion his mind was invaded by a series of pictures, like slides put into a projector at random, out of sequence. Phrases came back to him, often meaningless, always out of context.

Debbie Joyce lying on the tiled floor, her black hair almost hiding the unspeakable things which had happened to her face.

'Debbie liked to set the pace—'

'You got the impression sometimes that she took a delight in hurting people.'

'Why did she marry me? I asked myself that question many times during each day and night that we were together and I still do not know the answer.'

Elaine Bennett. Her body too was crumpled up on a tiled floor. She too, had dark hair.

Both girls were twenty-five years old.

One thing seemed certain, the killer was not a homicidal maniac killing at random.

Sleep came at last, it must have done, for the next thing he knew was being awakened by Helen with a cup of coffee.

'It's eight o'clock.'

# CHAPTER FOUR

The information Wycliffe had given to the press was
necessarily scanty and it made headline news only in
the local paper. The London dailies gave it a paragraph
in the stop press. But this was the lull before the storm.
Once the reporters had had time to dig around, the
'City of Fear' or something like it would be on every
front page. Two killings and an abortive attack were
more than enough to resurrect Jack the Ripper.

Mr Bellings, the deputy chief, always sensitive to
publicity of any kind, looked in on Wycliffe to say that
they must be careful not to foster a mood of hysteria on
the strength of two killings. Wycliffe suggested that he
might like to issue a statement but Mr Bellings was too
astute to be caught that way. 'I have every confidence
in your discretion, Charles.'

Meanwhile routine work went ahead. An industria-
list chemist was preparing a number of pieces of
material very lightly impregnated with various
solvents and resins for Valerie to smell. The area where
the attack on her had been made, fenced off and
guarded through the night, was now being thoroughly
studied and searched. Through the night also the flat in
Edgcumbe Close had been explored in meticulous
detail. The detectives' reports were on Wycliffe's desk,
so were reports from the pathologist and from forensic.

They amounted to very little, no new information. The killer had left no identifiable trademark and, what was equally important, Elaine Bennett, like Debbie Joyce, seemed to have lived only from day to day. No letters, no mementoes to shed light on her twenty-five years of life. Debbie, at least had her professional photographs. Wycliffe could only marvel at the way these young people lived their complex lives out of a suitcase when his continuing sense of individuality seemed to depend on a lorry load of books, papers, photographs, notebooks, ornaments and pictures. But Mr and Mrs Bennett had come over from Paignton during the night and he was hopeful that they might fill some of the gaps.

W.P.C. Saxton came in with another batch of reports. Her blue uniform, a faultless fit, looked as though it had just come off a Hartnell peg; her ash-blonde hair was like 'after' in the shampoo advertisements and her skin, even in this winter weather, was slightly tanned. Sometimes he almost wished her on Bellings who coped with a middle-aged dragon. He was unintentionally brusque.

'Do you live at home?'

'No, sir, I live in lodgings during the week but I go home most weekends.'

'Have you kept a lot of things from your childhood and schooldays—books, school reports, photographs —that sort of thing?'

She showed no surprise. 'No, sir, that's what mothers do, isn't it? My mother has a hoard of such stuff from my first pair of shoes onwards.' She hovered. 'If you're thinking of Elaine Bennett, sir, I doubt if you've found much in her flat but I wouldn't mind betting that her mother will have a real store of this sort of thing.' She smiled.

W.P.C. Burden had been given the job of visiting the hospital and breaking the news to Valerie Hughes. Sue Burden was the same age as the girls, pleasant, homely and, by nature, sympathetic.

'You mean that after he left me he went to the flat and ...' Valerie's brow wrinkled in an effort of comprehension. 'I can't believe it, truly, I can't.' She sat, propped up by pillows, staring at the foot of the bed.

'I mean, why Elaine?'

'That's what we've got to find out.'

'This other girl, Debbie Joyce, I mean, girls like that ask for it, don't they?'

'How well did you know Elaine?'

A shrewd look from the blue eyes. 'We've shared a flat for over a year.'

'What sort of girl was she?'

'We got on.'

'Did she have a regular boyfriend?'

A small smile which quickly faded. 'There was a boy called Nigel Sears but he was just one in a long line. It wasn't serious.'

'Doing the rounds?'

'She had a regular boy a few months back. I thought she was going to settle down but something went wrong.' A thoughtful pause. 'Elaine hated the idea of being tied to anything or anybody. I mean, that's why she gave up the hospital. And it was the same with boys.'

'Sleeping around?'

'A bit.'

'Names?'

'What do you take me for?'

'We've got to know about her if there's to be any chance of finding the chap who killed her.'

A solemn nod. 'I suppose so. In any case it makes no difference now.'

But what she knew amounted to very little, a few Christian names, the makes of one or two cars owned by Elaine's boyfriends.

'Elaine knew that Debbie had been murdered?'

'We heard it on the telly last night at six o'clock.'

'Did she say anything which suggested that she knew the girl?'

'Oh, she knew her all right, they were quite friendly when they were at school.'

'You mean that they went to school together?'

'No, I don't know the details but they didn't go to the same school, I think they met playing inter-schools hockey.'

'But in that case Elaine would have known her as Rosaline Parkin, and that name wasn't mentioned yesterday.'

'No, but she'd seen her since, at the Golden Cockerel, and recognised her.'

'Was Elaine a regular at the Golden Cockerel?'

'I don't know about a regular but I think she went there fairly often.'

'Did she seem very surprised or shocked when she heard about the murder?'

Valerie frowned, trying hard to be objective. 'No, I don't think so. She said something about it being no wonder she got murdered, considering the way she carried on at the club.'

'What did she mean by that?'

'I don't know. I doubt if she meant very much, Elaine liked to appear as though she had inside information about anything that happened.'

'Did you have the impression that she herself felt threatened?'

Valerie shook her head decisively, then regretted it because of the pain it caused. 'No, I don't think the idea entered her mind; I'm quite sure it didn't.'

They were silent for a time while Valerie sipped an orange drink.

'She didn't talk about herself much and rarely mentioned the past. Her father and mother were a bit of a drag, kind and all that, thought the world of her but over-protective, if you know what I mean. Not like mine—"Get out and get on with it, girl!" She had quite a good education, she took "A"-levels and she was an S.R.N., I'm only state enrolled. She'd have been a sister by now if she'd stayed with the hospital.' She shivered. 'God, I can't take it in that she's gone.'

Sue Burden reported to Chief Inspector Gill who told her that she was to take charge of Elaine Bennett's parents. 'Go back with them to Paignton or wherever it is they come from, find out what you can.'

'The trouble is, sir, I haven't a clue what it is I'm supposed to do.'

Gill put on his baby-frightening smile. 'Simple! Find out why she got herself strangled and who did it. If her mother is like most, she'll talk, all you've got to do is pin your ears back and ask the right questions. You'll also go through the girl's belongings and all the stuff her mother keeps.'

The W.P.C. frowned. 'But I don't see where it's likely to get us, sir. Surely it's obvious the man's a nutter, he wouldn't have had a *reason* for killing her, not a real motive.'

Gill grinned. 'No thinking in the ranks. Run along now and get on with it.'

She met the Bennetts and got them into a police car. He was tall and thin and pale; she was dumpy, not to say fat; and normally, one would think, cheerful. Now her cheeks were stained with tears and she had an unhealthy flush.

'She was such a good girl. Why would anybody want to . . . ?'

They accepted the young policewoman without seeming to notice her. When they reached their bungalow in Paignton, which had a view of the sea, they let her make them a cup of tea and, later, they were persuaded to eat a little of the omelette she made from cheese and eggs. Mr Bennett hovered over her as she worked in the kitchen.

'Mother's taken it very hard.' But, if anything, he was more distraught than his wife.

Unable to stay at his desk for long, Wycliffe drove out to the allotments. He approached from Godolphin Road, a fairly wide, straight road lined with semi-detached villas built between the wars. Most of them had lapwood fencing and a few shrubs in the gardens. There was a bus stop every three hundred yards or so and a telephone kiosk on a patch of waste ground where the path across the allotments joined the road. It was not an arterial road but carried a fair amount of traffic between the city and large housing developments in its eastern suburbs.

The allotments presented a bleak prospect, a biting wind swept across the almost bare soil, rattling the corrugated iron sheeting of the ugly little sheds. Policemen stood about, waiting to be of use to the experts, stamping their feet and flailing their arms to keep warm. Sergeant Smith, the sour photographer, stalked about with his cameras and cursed steadily. Gill was sitting in a patrol car by the constable on radio watch. Wycliffe got into the back seat.

'Anything?'

Gill twisted round in his seat. 'It's obvious where he stood waiting, a gap in the privet hedge. The ground is well trodden but there are no identifiable footprints. He must take a size nine or ten in shoes which means that he's no midget. Of course, we've collected an assortment of litter but there's only one item which might be useful.' He reached into the glove tray of the car and produced a transparent polythene envelope containing a smaller manilla envelope which had a little window near the top. 'It was found where he was standing. As you see, it was crumpled and it's possible that he pulled it out of his pocket with his handkerchief. Of course, it may be nothing to do with him . . .'

'What is it—a wages packet?'

'I think so. The pay card fits in so that the man's name shows through the window. If it did come from his pocket it might help.'

'I'll take this.'

'It hasn't been checked for dabs.'

'I know.'

Gill grinned. 'In any case it's a job for a D.C.'

'I know that, too. They get the best of it, don't they?' That, to a point, was genuine. As rank had separated him more and more from the spadework—and foot-work—of detection, he had felt increasingly frustrated. It would have been absurd to pretend that he did not welcome the chance to direct investigations instead of accepting direction from others but he still envied the men who worked at the level where it all happened. Occasionally, as now, he broke out.

He drove to a firm of wholesale stationers who had their offices in the city centre and was taken to the manager.

The manager only glanced at the envelope. 'No, Mr Wycliffe, we don't supply them, I wish we did.' He reached down a catalogue and flicked through the pages. 'Here we are, they're made by Deacon and Hall, part of a wages system which they supply. As far as I know there are three firms in the city using the system. The biggest is Pneumax, they make compressors and compressed air equipment. They must be the largest employers in the city; then there is Magnelec, the radio and television people, with about a thousand or fifteen hundred on their pay-roll and, finally, Goosens who assemble Italian typewriters and business machines under licence, they employ three or four hundred. The envelopes are supplied in the flat. Wages clerks lay the computer print-out on the envelope with the correct number of notes and the machine folds and seals them.'

'What about coin?'

'They don't pay coin. They have an agreement with the unions to pay to the nearest pound and carry for-ward balances.'

He was tempted to continue playing truant and to visit the three firms but his conscience got the better of him and he returned to his office and set a detective constable to work.

There were two reports in his tray amounting to new evidence. Valerie Hughes had sniffed the chemist's array of lightly impregnated fabrics and picked out turpentine as the perfume of the month. Wycliffe had little faith in the outcome but he gave instructions for the three firms using the Deacon and Hall wages system to be questioned about the use of turpentine in any of their technical processes. The other item seemed more promising. In response to an appeal on the local radio a woman had come forward who had been in Marshfield Road shortly after the time at which Elaine Bennett must have been murdered. Marshfield Road is the alternative, longer route from Edgcumbe Close to Godolphin Road.

'I was taking the dog for a little walk, poor thing, he'd been cooped up all day. Just to the main road and back. As I was coming back down the road, not far from my house, I saw this man. He was hurrying along, half running and I thought to myself he must be wanting to catch a bus in Godolphin Road. In the evenings they're few and far between.'

'Did you get a good look at him?'

'Not a good look. For one thing he was on the other side of the road but he passed under a street lamp and I could see him plain enough.'

'What did he look like?'

'Well, it's hard to say. I mean, he was just ordinary looking.'

'Tall or short, thin or fat?'

'Oh, tall and not fat. He had this long mackintosh which looked as though it was wet through and through. It was clinging about his legs.'

'Was he wearing a hat?'

'Yes, I think he had some sort of hat. I think it was a cap but I'm not sure.'

'Old or young?'

'Well, I don't know but I got the impression he wasn't a youngster. It went through my mind that he must be pretty fit hurrying like that and I wouldn't have thought that if he'd been a young man, would I?'

'Glasses?'

'I don't think so. I'd have noticed if he had.'

'You saw his face?'

'Well, I must have done but I can't tell you what he looked like.'

'Were there any cars parked along Marshfield Road at this time?'

'There are always cars parked there and especially at night, people are too lazy to put their cars away and they leave them in the street.'

'Could this man you saw have been running towards a parked car and not to a bus stop in Godolphin Road?'

She hesitated. 'I suppose so, but what would have been the point of running? He was wet enough already.'

'Did you hear a car start after he passed you?'

'I might have done, I can't really say one way or the other.'

Not much but decidedly something. The bus stop where Marshfield Road joined Godolphin Road was the one before the allotments and it might be possible to get something from a conductor or driver on the route.

Whenever Wycliffe was working at headquarters he lunched at Teague's, an old-fashioned eating house, narrow, little more than a broad passage between a supermarket and a bank. Two lines of high-backed booths separated by a matted walk, a set meal each day, well prepared. There was an atmosphere of calm, almost of reverence, and people conversed in low voices as though in church. There were groups of two, three or four people, regulars, who always sat in the same booth and though each group must have been well known to all the others they rarely exchanged more than a brief nod in passing. It had taken some time to convert Gill to Teague's, and even longer for him to moderate his voice and manner to the prevailing standards.

They did not have to give an order; the waitress brought Wycliffe a lager, Gill a draught beer then the soup of the day followed by the main course.

'I've put Sue Burden on dealing with the Bennett parents,' Gill said. 'She's been with them most of the morning and now she's gone back to Paignton with them.'

'She knows what she's looking for?'

Gill shrugged. 'A motive? Links between the two girls? Her guess is as good as mine. She won't find anything, the chap is a nutter and short of a fluke we shan't get him until he gets careless and starts to show off.'

Wycliffe sipped his lager. 'He's rational to the extent that he chooses his victims; any girl won't do. He was obviously concerned about Valerie Hughes, so concerned that he seems to have telephoned the hospital for news of her.'

Gill shook his head. 'It comes to the same thing in the end. They may start by rationalising what they do but finally it comes down to what it is, the lust to kill. In any case, on what criteria does he choose his victims? As likely as not it's the colour of their hair or the way they wriggle their backsides when they walk.' He grimaced and startled a passing waitress. 'The fact is that no girl will be safe until the bastard is locked up.'

There was sense in what Gill said, sense based on experience but Wycliffe did not agree with him.

As they were returning to the office after lunch the afternoon edition of *The News* was already on the streets and the placards asked a succinct question:

MADMAN ON THE LOOSE?

Wycliffe and Gill were making their way among the crowds of people returning to work; everybody was in a hurry, shoulders hunched against the biting wind. There was little opportunity for talk but Gill was like a dog with a bone.

'Night patrols and decoy girls, that's the only answer to this kind of thing.'

Wycliffe was placatory. 'We may come to that, Jimmy, but we don't want to exhaust our resources just waiting for something to happen.'

The bus station enquiry was productive. At 10.05 the previous evening a conductor on a 622 bus out of the city had noticed a man near the bus stop at the junction of Marshfield and Godolphin Roads. For what it was worth the conductor's description tallied with the woman's. Tall, middle-aged to oldish, wearing a mackintosh and cap, he was hurrying in the same direction as the bus was travelling.

'We passed him before the stop and at the stop I waited for him to catch up thinking he wanted to get on.'

'But he didn't?'

'He just went by as though the bus wasn't there. I don't think he noticed.'

'What did he look like?'

'I can't tell you more than I have. The only light came from the bus and when you're standing in the light you can't see much of anything beyond it.'

A middle-aged man, fairly tall, taking size nine in shoes and active for his age. He worked for one of the three firms who used the Deacon and Hall wages system and he had recently been in contact with turpentine.

Wycliffe smiled to himself. If only it were that simple. Such a summary assumed that witnesses were accurate, that all the facts referred to the same man and that that man was a killer. Going along with the idea however, Wycliffe would have added to the list of attributes one which he regarded as important, the man had a conscience.

Nigel Sears, Elaine Bennett's current boyfriend, had been found; he was an electrician working for a firm of contractors and Gill had him picked up.

He was stocky, bullet-headed, upset and scared.

'You've heard?'

'One of my mates showed it me in the paper.' He sat, fidgeting, not knowing what to do with his hands.

'She was your girl friend; was it serious?'

'Not exactly serious; we didn't aim to get married or anything like that.'

'Why not?'

The boy shifted uncomfortably. 'Well, it wasn't like that. For one thing, Elaine had other boyfriends. I mean, I wasn't the only one.'

'Like that, was she?'

He flushed. 'She wasn't like anything, she just hadn't settled down to one bloke yet.'

'All right, don't shout at me, lad. Did you go to bed with her?'

'Once or twice.'

'And the others—did they?'

'I don't know, do I? I wasn't the first.'

'You've got a Mini, haven't you?'

'Yes, why?'

'Clapped out?'

'She's six years old, but —'.

'You'd have done better with Elaine if you'd had a Jag, is that it?'

He reddened again. 'I don't see what you're getting at.'

'She liked a good time?'

'Is there anything wrong with that?'

'Ever heard of Debbie Joyce?'

'I heard that she had been found dead in her flat.'

'But before that?'

'I knew that she was a singer at the Cock.'

'So you're one of that lot, are you?'

Sears was resentful. 'I'm not one of any lot, I've been to the Cock twice.'

'With Elaine?'

'Yes, she wanted to go there but it isn't my sort of place. Too pricey for one thing.'

'Did Elaine know Debbie—apart from seeing her at the club?'

His forehead wrinkled. 'I think she might have done.'

'Think?'

'I'm pretty sure. After her act Debbie would change then come and join the customers—you know the routine. The first night I was there I thought she was coming to our table but she changed her mind and sheered off. Elaine said, "She knows better than come here", but she wouldn't tell me what she meant.'

Gill glared in silence at the young man for some time, then he said, 'O.K. That'll do for now but don't go swanning off to Majorca without saying good-bye.'

Gill caught Wycliffe in a reflective mood. He was standing by the big window in his office, appparently mesmerised by the endless flow of the traffic.

'Two lads in their twenties, Debbie Joyce's sleeping partner and the latest of Elaine Bennett's boyfriends, neither of them killers, psychopathic or otherwise. These crimes are the work of a mature man.'

Gill tapped ash on to the carpet. 'I'm inclined to agree, and, on the menu so far we have Papa Bourg and Mr Matthew Norman. From what you say, Norman seems well qualified by background, temperament and experience to be a nutter and Bourg might do anything in the way of business.'

Wycliffe laughed despite himself. 'Neither of them has a weekly wage packet and Bourg certainly isn't tall and thin. All the same, I agree that they should be checked out.'

'I'll have a word with Norman this afternoon.'

'Leave it to Scales.'

Gill grinned amiably. 'You think I might create a diplomatic incident?' He knew his limitations and accepted them.

'Could be. Seriously, I can see the possibility that Norman might have killed his wife but there is no evidence of any connection between him and Elaine Bennett.'

'She used to be a nurse at Millfield.'

'So did hundreds of others.'

Reports were trickling in all the time.

Scales had established that the maiden aunt who had brought up Debbie Joyce or Rosaline Parkin, was dead. She had died of a heart atack two years before. Rosaline and her aunt had lived in a dreary little terraced house near the docks where the lorries rumbled past day and night. The neighbours were full of praise for the way in which the aunt had struggled to bring up her niece.

'And what thanks did she get, poor soul? As soon as she could keep herself young madam was off and never come near the place again in five years. Not but what that could have been a blessing in disguise for even when she was at school she was always in trouble. But she was back quick enough when the old lady died, selling up her bits and pieces.'

Another neighbour had a similar view.

'So she'd changed her name, had she. I read about a Debbie Joyce in the paper but I didn't know it was her. Well, I don't wish nobody any harm but you can't help feeling sometimes that there's a sort of justice in these things. She was always out for number one and she was that rude! I remember once when ... '

Detection commonly proceeds by laborious and exceedingly tedious processes of elimination which means that, at the end of an investigation, it is usually possible to look back through the reams of paper and to show that most of the work was wasted. Yet there is no other systematic approach. An inspired guess may sometimes save days of slogging but guesses are only inspired when they turn out to be right.

So the three firms who used the Deacon and Hall

wages system were persuaded to provide lists of the names, addresses and ages of all weekly paid male employees. When these lists were to hand detectives would go through them picking out the middle-aged and those who lived in the eastern suburbs. With these new, much shorter lists, they would attempt some further elimination, say, all those men under five feet eight in height which would mean seeing the men concerned. Almost certainly all of it would prove a waste of time. They would narrow the field to two or three perfectly harmless, middle-aged men whose wildest excess was a couple of pints at the local on a Saturday night.

# CHAPTER FIVE

Four or five days of almost continuous rain while the city sprawls under leaden clouds, its roofs and streets gleaming in the steely January light. Another two months of winter ahead. Then without warning, comes a golden day, the sun shines from a blue sky, the air seems to be filled with a luminous, golden haze, the buildings and streets have been washed clean and people smile at total strangers. A taste of spring and hope is reborn.

Wednesday was such a day and Wycliffe caught himself whistling as he waited patiently at a junction to join the main stream of traffic city bound. A long-haired youth in a Mini held back to let him in and he was so surprised that he missed his gear.

Sun streamed through his office window and W.P.C. Saxton had put a little cut-glass vase of snowdrops on his desk beside the daily papers. He glanced at the headlines with detachment as one does on holiday.

'Killer Terrorises City'; 'The Dangerous Age?'—a reference to the fact that the three girls attacked were twenty-five years old. 'M.P. Demands Vigilante Patrols'.

If Wycliffe was still in doubt about the kind of man he was looking for the crime reporters were not; a madman, a compulsive killer, a psychopath. One reporter claimed to have been reliably informed that young police women, in plain clothes, were acting as a bait in police traps, risking their lives each night in unfrequented streets and alleys. 'Despite the risks Chief Superintendent Wycliffe has more volunteers for the work than he can use.'

All to give the great British public a warm feeling inside to go with their cornflakes.

Against all this (and Jimmy Gill) Wycliffe's reasons for believing that he was dealing with a rational man and not a homicidal lunatic began to look thin. His only evidence was the killer's failure to finish what he had started with Valerie Hughes and the strong possibility that he had telephoned the hospital in some anxiety to find out how she was. If Wycliffe was right, the man had killed Debbie Joyce and Elaine Bennett either because they had done him some injury or because they threatened him in some way. What kind of injury? What kind of threat? Good questions. It came back to possible links between the two girls. They had not been to the same school. Debbie had passed her eleven-plus and gone to Cholsey Grammar while the Bennett's bakery had been sufficiently prosperous to send Elaine to Bishop Fuller's, a rather plush day-school for girls. But they had known each other as schoolgirls and been friendly for a time.

There was little prospect of identifying the killer on present evidence. Neither Mrs Burton, the witness in Marshfield Road, nor the conductor of the 622 bus could remember enough of the man they saw to make an identikit picture of any value. Medium height or tall, middle-aged or old, not fat, wearing a fawn or grey mackintosh and a cap. Added to that he probably took size nine in shoes and it was possible that he worked at one of the three concerns that used the Deacon and Hall wages system. That was all they had and no amount of suggestion or persuasion could make it more. All the same, detectives were touting this meagre description round the neighbourhood of Godolphin Road and a radio appeal had gone out for anyone who had seen such a man on Monday evening.

Wycliffe, still in search of his common denominator, had decided to begin with the two schools.

Cholsey Grammar had become Cholsey Comprehensive and they had moved into new buildings since Rosaline Parkin's day. A trim heap of glass-sided packing cases standing out like a very sore thumb in a semi-rural landscape on the northern outskirts of the city.

The headmaster had been reorganised with his school, but reluctantly, and Wycliffe could see in his office signs of reactionary nostalgia. Team photographs on the walls, an M.A. hood and gown behind the door and the Wadham crest on a wooden shield above the bookcase.

'I read in the newspaper what had happened to the poor girl. I remember her very well. She was dark and sallow, rather striking. Academically she was good but her background didn't help—no tradition of academic work. Of course, nowadays, we no longer expect it.' A profound sigh.

Wycliffe asked obvious questions and got obvious answers. The central heating made the room uncomfortably warm and with the sun shining on well-tended playing fields it could have been a summer's day. A teacher's voice droned monotonously in the next room and Wycliffe could imagine rows of children drowsing over their books.

'We are looking for a possible link between Rosaline and the other girl who was killed—Elaine Bennett. Elaine did not go to this school, she was a pupil at Bishop Fuller's.'

The headmaster ran a thin hand over his balding skull. 'I don't know her, of course.'

'Were there any organised contacts between the two schools—games, excursions, that sort of thing?'

'There used to be, certainly. The girls played them at hockey and, now I come to think of it, Rosaline was a good little hockey player, a winger, very fast. And that reminds me of another thing, she had fits.'

'Fits?'

'She was epileptic and she had a fit once on the hockey field. We felt that she should give up games but the school doctor said that she must be allowed to carry on a normal life.'

It is difficult to frame questions when you have no idea of what it is you are trying to find out.

'What sort of girl was she—rebellious? Conformist?' The headmaster scratched his chin. 'It was a good many years ago, remember, but as far as I can recall she was neither one nor the other. Some children, not necessarily the most worthwhile, fit into school like a hand into a glove. Rosaline was not one of those but I don't recall her as a trouble maker either.'

He frowned in an effort of recollection then reached for his internal telephone.

'I'll ask my deputy to join us, her memory is more dependable than mine.'

Miss Finch came in and was introduced. She was aptly named, her movements were quick and darting like those of a small, slightly pugnacious bird. She was plump and fiftyish with the clear skin which is sometimes the prize of life-long celibacy.

'Rosaline Parkin? I remember her very well. I saw in this morning's paper that it was she who was killed in those new flats.'

'I was saying to the superintendent that she was an intelligent girl and not, as I remember, the sort to be in trouble.'

Miss Finch smiled. 'Not the sort to be found out certainly. In my experience she was dangerous, a very bad influence in the school and usually clever enough to escape the consequences of her actions.'

The headmaster looked crestfallen. 'Indeed? I am surprised.'

'Surely you remember the trouble she caused on one of those vacation trips that Miss Russell organised?'

'What sort of trouble?' Mildly, from Wycliffe.

Miss Finch frowned. 'It was before my appointment as deputy head but I was here on the staff. A Miss Russell was deputy and she organised a lot of out-of-school activities. On this occasion she took a party of girls, drawn from several schools, to a hostel in Dorset for three weeks during the summer vacation. They were to experience the advantages of communal living of which, as day-school pupils, they had been deprived.' Miss Finch's lip curled.

'What happened?'

'I did not hear all the details. Miss Russell dealt with the matter herself but I do know that the parents of a girl from another school complained that their daughter had been harassed and bullied by a group of girls of whom Rosaline Parkin was the ringleader. There was a good deal of very unpleasant gossip.' Miss Finch paused and smoothed the skirt of her Jaeger two-piece. 'I'm afraid it emerged that the whole trip had been something of a disaster and Miss Russell could not entirely escape responsibility.'

'What happened to the girl—to Rosaline?'

Miss Finch pursed her lips. 'Nothing happened to her. She was not punished in any way.'

The headmaster was embarrassed. 'Now you mention it I do remember there was a complaint from a parent which I passed to Miss Russell. I had no idea that it had turned out to be as serious as you say.'

Miss Finch shrugged. 'That *is* interesting. I had supposed that Miss Russell would keep you informed.'

'Do you remember the name of the parents who complained?'

'No, I do not, nor the school from which the child

came. Like most things in school it was a nine-day wonder.'

'Perhaps some other member of your staff?'

'I think it very unlikely, there are only two or three of us left from the old days.'

'This Miss Russell, did she leave to take up another appointment?'

The headmaster nodded. 'Oh, yes, a school somewhere near Cambridge. I could look it up if it is of any interest to you.'

Miss Finch intervened. 'No need. She went as deputy head to Lady Margaret's near Huntingdon. She was very fortunate to get such an appointment, very fortunate indeed.'

Wycliffe stood up. 'Perhaps you will have a word with other members of staff who were here when Rosaline was a pupil and telephone me if there is anything further you can tell me.'

The headmaster escorted him to the main entrance through hordes of children swarming the corridors during a change of lessons.

The atmosphere at Bishop Fuller's was different. Miss Buckley, the headmistress, had her office in the Georgian mansion which formed the nucleus of the school. A shabbily elegant room with panelled walls, glass-fronted bookcases and tall windows.

'Elaine Bennett—when you telephoned I got out her file.' She fingered a blue folder on her desk. 'Of course I heard what had happened to her and I imagine that is why you are here.'

A few minutes introductory fencing.

'She was not a particularly able girl—five Ordinary level passes but she failed her Advanced levels.'

'What about her as a person?'

A miniscule shrug. 'She was not a popular girl either with her contemporaries or with the staff. Over-indulgent parents. Elaine behaved as though she had a prescriptive right to special treatment. Needless to say, she didn't get it here.' No false sentiment with Miss Buckley.

'Did she play hockey?'

He received the what-have-I-missed-here look and Miss Buckley put on her library spectacles to refer to the file. 'Yes, she did, she was a member of our first team.'

'Would she have been likely to have played in matches against Cholsey Grammar?'

Another inquisitive glance. 'Presumably, since that was one of the schools on our fixture list at that time.'

'Can you tell me if she took part in any joint excursions or school visits with girls from Cholsey?'

Miss Buckley did not conceal her impatience. 'Really, superintendent, we are dealing with events which occurred nine or ten years ago. It is quite likely that she would have taken part in joint school activities, we did a great deal of that sort of thing.'

'But you have no records?'

'Good heavens, no! I suppose it's just possible that something of the sort might have been mentioned in her testimonial.'

Again a reference to the file.

'Yes, as it happens there is something here. Her house-mistress says that she took part in our German exchange programme, if that is of any interest.'

'Nothing else?'

'Nothing here.'

'Does the name Rosaline Parkin mean anything to you?'

She frowned. 'Wasn't that the real name of the girl who was murdered in the Grenville flats? I think I saw it in the paper this morning.'

'Apart from that?'

'She was not a pupil here.' For Miss Buckley that closed the subject.

A bell rang and he became aware of a rising tide of movement through the building and beyond.

'Rosaline was a pupil at Cholsey while Elaine was here.'

Miss Buckley was unimpressed. 'I think I see your drift, superintendent, but surely it is unlikely that events so far back should have any significance now.'

Wycliffe ignored that one. 'Presumably there are members of your staff who were here in Elaine's day?'

'Of course, most of them. We are a very stable institution.'

Of course. That was what middle-grade executives and prosperous trades people paid for and skimped to do it. Stability and tradition.

'Then perhaps you would ask them if they remember any occasion when, in joint activities with Cholsey, something notable occurred involving Elaine?' It sounded thin, thin as railway soup.

'Notable? In what way?'

Wycliffe sympathised with pupils of Miss Buckley's faced with her uncompromising specificity.

'I've no idea, probably something unpleasant, perhaps something which might have given rise to a deeply felt grievance.'

Miss Buckley closed Elaine's file. 'I doubt if they will be able to help but I will do as you ask.'

Wycliffe drove back to his headquarters through streets transformed by the winter sunshine. People strolled along the pavements and there were gossiping groups at the street corners. The women were dressed more colourfully and the whole population seemed to be a little high, mildly intoxicated by the warmth and the golden light.

On his desk a report summarised the conclusions of the detectives who had worked on the lists provided by the three firms using the Deacon and Hall wages system.

1. The three firms between them employ 3,600 persons.

2. 2,928 are paid weekly and of these 1,974 are men.
3. 953 of the men are over forty years of age and 521 are over 45.
4. The individuals in the second category of 3 are being further investigated.

Wycliffe turned to W.P.C. Saxton who was waiting to deal with the post. 'When I was at school it was all about filling a bath from two taps with the plug out.'

'Sir?'

'Never mind.'

Five hundred and twenty-one men. If one of them took size nine in shoes, was tall, thin and active and smelt of turpentine, then God help him.

Lies, damned lies and statistics. Wycliffe's sentiments exactly.

Despite the euphoric effect of the weather he was not optimistic about the case. Unless the killer made some further move . . .

He got a copy of an Educational Year Book and looked up Lady Margaret's School which the knowledgeable Miss Finch had said was near Huntingdon. He found it. Lady Margaret's School for Girls, Lynfield House, near Huntingdon. 650 girls. Boarding with some day pupils. Headmistress: Miss D.M. Lester-Brown, M.A., B.Lit., Oxon.

He telephoned and after some brief negotiation spoke with Miss Lester-Brown.

'Miss Russell? Miss Dorothy Russell? Yes, I remember her very well.' The headmistress was suave, courteous and guarded. Even over the telephone he could sense that Miss Lester-Brown was marshalling her defences. 'No, she is not with us now, unfortunately she stayed with us for only one year . . . She resigned . . . No, as far as I know she did not leave to take up another teaching post . . . No, I have no idea what she did . . . In her letter of resignation she mentioned personal reasons . . . No, I am afraid that I do not have her present address.'

'Thank you,' Wycliffe muttered as he put down the receiver.

Perhaps after all there was light ahead.

He picked up the telephone again and asked to be put through to the Headmaster of Cholsey Comprehensive.

'Wycliffe again. I'm sorry. This Miss Russell who was once your deputy, when she was appointed you must have had a good deal of information about her—her background, where she came from, that sort of thing . . .'

The headmaster muttered something about confidentiality. Wycliffe was as bland as milk.

'I quite understand but all I want is to get in touch with her . . . No, she is not still at Huntingdon and they have no idea what has happened to her. It is, or could be, very important indeed. If you could tell me her home town it might help—where she went to school.'

Reluctant assent. 'It will take me some time to find the papers, after all it was several years ago.'

'You will ring me back?'

'As soon as I can.'

'One more thing, don't teachers have service numbers?'

'They do, indeed.'

'Then perhaps you would let me have hers.'

Bread upon the waters.

He made one more telephone call, to Huntingdon C.I.D., asking them to make discreet enquiries concerning Miss Russell's stay at Lady Margaret's.

He lunched at Teague's and returned to deal with some of the accumulated paper-work. His industry earned the approval of W.P.C. Saxton who worried about it more than he did.

The Headmaster of Cholsey Comprehensive telephoned with the information he had requested. Miss Russell had been appointed in 1960 and she had left in

1966. Before coming to Cholsey she had held appointments in Surrey and Bristol.

'Where was she at school, herself?'

'The Celia Ayrton Grammar School for Girls, near Lincoln. She left in 1944 to go up to Cambridge.'

'And her service number?'

The headmaster gave it.

Wycliffe telephoned the Department of Education asking for news of Miss Russell and spoke to a gloomy official who took a poor view of his enquiry and told him that it could only be considered if it came through the Home Office. Finally he put through a call to Lincoln C.I.D. for any information they could give him about Miss Russell and her family.

By the time W.P.C. Saxton left at half-past five, the mound of paper had been reduced to manageable proportions. He lit a pipe and stood by his window watching the home-going traffic. It was dark and the sky had remained clear so there was frost in the air. Everything sparkled, the car lights seemed brighter, more intense, the scene was vivid, cheerful, purposeful; these people were going home to wives, families, sweethearts, after a day's work. No longer did he murmur as he watched them, 'Futile!'

He was about to leave himself when the telephone rang.

'The editor of *The News* for you, sir.'

'Put him through.'

They were old acquaintances and both understood the rules of the game.

'I've a note here which purports to come from the killer, chief superintendent. I shall print it, of course but, as always, I want to co-operate. It's too late tonight but it will appear in our morning editions. I thought you might like to see it first.'

'I'll be over.'

The last edition was going out on the streets and the

building was almost deserted. In the editor's office he was offered sherry.

'When we saw what it was we didn't maul it.'

The note lay in a polythene cover on the editor's desk and the envelope, crumpled and evidently rescued from the wastepaper basket, was beside it. The note and the address on the envelope had been written in block capitals using a soft pencil and the paper of the note was thick and of coarse texture like duplicating paper. The writing was neat and the message clear and concise:

I DO NOT WANT TO TERRORISE PEOPLE. THEY SAY THAT I AM A PSYCHOPATHIC KILLER BUT THIS IS NOT TRUE. IF I HAD BEEN I WOULD HAVE KILLED THE WRONG GIRL ON MONDAY NIGHT. THE WOMEN WHO DIED ARE TWO OF THE GUILTY ONES. PEOPLE CANNOT DESTROY LIVES OF OTHERS WITHOUT BEING PUNISHED.

The editor looked at Wycliffe with the air of one who, having delivered the goods, expects to see the colour of the other chap's money.

'What's all this about the wrong girl?'

'Presumably he made a mistake in attacking Valerie Hughes and when he discovered his mistake he let her go.'

'You knew this?'

'It was a possibility.'

'And Elaine Bennett was the right girl?'

'Presumably.'

'Why?'

'I've no idea.'

The editor was chagrined or pretended to be. 'If you would rather have your chaps followed round by reporters . . . '

Wycliffe said nothing.

'It looks as though this fellow is working off some sort of vendetta.'

'Perhaps. When did you get this?'

'It was delivered by hand to our street office before they closed at five-thirty this evening.'

'You mean that it was handed over the counter?'

'No, it was pushed through the letter box. One of the girls noticed it in the little wire cage when she was locking up. I've had a photostat done so you can take the original.'

Wycliffe nodded. 'This is obviously a reply to what you and others printed this morning.'

'Are you prepared to comment on what he has to say?'

'No, but thanks for the letter and the sherry.'

'They were both investments,' the editor said.

Back in his office Wycliffe treated the note very seriously. The note and the envelope were photographed then sent at once to forensic where they would be minutely examined and made to yield every scrap of information which they held. But he did not expect much. Here was a man who realised that block capitals give very little away. It is a waste of time to cut letters out of newspapers. A man with that much sense would be unlikely to give himself away through elementary carelessness.

Wycliffe sat at his desk with only the green-shaded desk lamp alight. He had not drawn the curtains over the big window behind him and the headlights of passing cars made wild patterns on the ceiling and walls. The subdued light fell on his blotter and on a photostat of the killer's declaration.

THE WOMEN WHO DIED ARE TWO OF THE GUILTY ONES.

Specific, unambiguous. You had to take this man seriously, to believe him, to believe at least that he meant what he wrote at the time of writing it.

They were not dealing with an indiscriminate killer, that much was confirmed.

THE WOMEN WHO DIED . . .

Debbie Joyce and Elaine Bennett were both twenty-five years old. How had they harmed a middle-aged man? Wycliffe was more than ever convinced that he was middle-aged or older; these were not the crimes of youth.

PEOPLE CANNOT DESTROY THE LIVES OF OTHERS WITHOUT BEING PUNISHED.

Perhaps it was not the killer himself who had been harmed but someone he loved. He saw himself as meting out justice.

He was right about a common denominator but had he been right in going back to the girls' schooldays? At least they knew each other at school. It was imperative now to follow that lead both through the schools and in the later lives of the girls.

TWO OF THE GUILTY ONES . . .

The implication was that there were others.

Finally, I AM NOT A PSYCHOPATHIC KILLER.

The need to defend himself drove him to the risky business of writing to *The News*. He could not bear to be misjudged even in anonymity.

As he stared at the note Wycliffe began to see a vague picture through the eye of his mind. Tall, lean, fastidious, gentle . . . Gentle! Yes, in spite of everything. A man to whom something had happened so devastating that he is completely thrown off balance, knocked off the rails. He has to rationalise his tragedy and, justly or unjustly, apportion the blame. It is in this process that he becomes obsessed.


For the past six months he had lodged with his sister and her husband in their little flat at the top of the *Guardian* building which Albert, his brother-in-law, called their penthouse.

He went up in the lift, took off his mackintosh and put it on a hanger in the hall cupboard.

'Is that you, Jim?'

His sister. Always the same welcome.

107

He went into his bedroom to wash and change his jacket.

Although he had lived there only half a year his room had acquired a distinctive character. There was a neat row of his books on the chest of drawers and two photographs in silver frames, one of a rather plain girl with short, straight hair and the other of a middle-aged woman with large, sad eyes. On the walls were reproductions of famous paintings, Vermeer, Canaletto, Hobbema.

He went into the living room which had a tiny dining alcove where the table was laid for the evening meal and Albert was already in his place. The television was on and the news had just started. The economic situation, a row in the U.N., a strike, the divorce of a famous actress.

Alice pushed two plates of pie through the hatch. 'You two get started, I'll be there in a minute.'

Albert was a stocky little man with black, curly hair and features which seemed to have been made of lumps of plasticene. He always looked very serious and solemn but he had a puckish sense of humour and Alice said that he ought to have been a clown.

'How's gaffer, Jim?'

'All right.' He could never accustom himself to Albert's familiarity. He was a formal person and though he did not resent his brother-in law's manner it embarrassed him because he could not reply in kind.

Alice came in with her plate. The general news had ended and the regional news began.

' . . . tension is mounting in the city. A spokesman at police headquarters said today that the possibility of further attacks could not be excluded. While there was no cause for panic it was hoped that young women in particular would behave sensibly and not go about alone or in unfrequented parts of the city after dark.'

'Terrible!' Alice said. 'Makes you afraid to put your face outside the door.'

Albert chuckled. 'You don't have to worry, old girl, he's after tender meat.'

The meal came to an end and Alice went to make coffee. Albert became serious.

'You thought any more about what I said to you?'

'Not really.'

'Of course it's your business but there's no sense leaving a house like that and nobody living in it—costing you money and nothing coming in.'

'I'll have to think about it.'

'Eighteen thousand, perhaps more, Freddie Miller reckoned you'd get, easy as falling off a log. Eighteen thousand at seven per cent free of tax would be over a thousand a year—a nice bit of extra. Or you could use your capital to expand the business.'

Jim said nothing and after a little while Albert tried again.

'If you're really determined not to sell you could let. I mean there must be some good tenants and you could pick and choose. I mean, it's not as though you was thinking of getting married again . . . '

'I've got to live somewhere.' He gestured vaguely. 'I mean, given time, when I've got used to the idea I might go back.'

'On your own in a house that size? And there's the rates—going up all the time.'

'Yes, the rates are high.'

'There you are! I mean, it doesn't make sense, does it?'

'I'll think about it.'

Alice came in with the coffee.

'I was just saying to Jim about the house—'

Alice frowned. 'Oh, leave it, Albert. It's Jim's business after all.' She picked up the newspaper. 'What's on the telly?'

Looking back Wycliffe could point to a moment in each of his major cases when he had experienced an abrupt change of outlook, achieved a fresh point of view, and a new *gestalt*. It was the moment when he ceased to be a detached investigator and became involved, seeing the case from the inside. Helen, his wife, and his close colleagues never failed to observe the change in him even if they did not understand its cause. He became reserved, taciturn, brusque, he rarely went home for meals and he walked a great deal hardly ever taking his car from the park except to go home at night.

In the present case the change came while he was sitting at his desk that evening, staring at the photostat of the killer's message to the press.

He picked up the telephone and asked for his home number.

'Is that you? I ought to have rung before, I'm afraid I shan't be home for a meal.'

'Now he tells me!'

'Sorry.'

'When shall I see you?'

'Probably lateish. Don't wait up.'

He put back the receiver with a feeling of release. It was odd but it was not new.

He glanced up at the clock. Five minutes to seven. He got his overcoat, opened the case file and extracted a couple of photographs which he put in his pocket then he switched off the desk lamp and left. He went down the stairs, through the duty room and out through the swing doors. The duty officer called 'Good-night, sir', but received no answer.

It was certainly frosty, he pulled up the collar of his overcoat and walked quickly in the direction of the city centre. As he approached the centre he turned off up Middle Street which ran behind a block of departmental stores. It was a remnant of the pre-war city and on the corner at the far end there was a pub which he had visited once or twice before. The frontage was faced with ornate green and buff tiles and the windows were frosted with elaborate scroll patterns. The Market

Arms. During the day it was popular with people from the pannier market but at night there was a select clientele made up of shop-keepers and tradesmen who still lived in the district.

Wycliffe unbuttoned his overcoat and took his beer and sandwiches to a little tile-topped table near the stove. Close by four men were playing whist for penny points. They took it in turn to examine Wycliffe with sidelong glances. Men in their forties and fifties who made enough to live in reasonable comfort and security without being affluent.

The fat man with a red face and an enormous signet ring was dealing. He seemed to obliterate the cards with his short fat fingers and he kept the tip of his tongue between his lips while he concentrated on the deal, like a child taking his first steps in drawing or writing. His partner was lean, colourless, with thinning grey hair and a straggly moustache stained with nicotine.

'Amy tells me your Joan is getting herself married.'

The fat man halted the deal. 'Saturday week at St Paul's. Chap who works in Finley's. He's only twenty-four but he's a buyer for their food hall. Done well for himself.'

'Might do a bit for you on the side.' The sally came from the third man, a bald, lugubrious individual who would have made a good undertaker. 'The odd box of oranges, a few trays of peaches off the back of the lorry.'

The fat man's face darkened. 'None of that, Sam, I run an honest business and always have.'

'No offence. Only a joke.'

'I hope so.'

They picked up their cards, counted them and found there had been a misdeal. They threw in, the fat man shuffled, baldy cut and the deal was restarted.

The fourth man who had not spoken so far, small dark with curly hair, said, 'There was hell up at my place before I left this evening. The wife wouldn't let

111

Tessa go out. Afraid she'd be picked up by the lunatic.'

'Quite right too,' the fat man said. 'It's a disgrace the way the police let these bloody perverts run loose. What are they paid for? As far as I can see all they bloody do is go to football on Saturday afternoons.'

'Can I get you another, superintendent?'

The landlord had come, diplomatically, to put coke on the stove. The message was not lost on the fat man who looked sheepishly at Wycliffe and received a blank stare in return.

There were three or four other tables occupied. One couple played draughts, the others sat, mostly in silence, drinking from time to time.

Why had he come here? He wanted a drink and a bit to eat, but why here? He asked himself the question and got only a vague answer. In fact he had formed a clearer picture of the man he wanted than he was prepared to admit. A solitary man, marked off from his fellows by events, but needing the reassurance of their presence. Where better than in a quiet pub like this one? He would not be among the card players but sitting alone, watching. If he was approached he would make an excuse ... But Wycliffe was the only one sitting alone in this bar. He shrugged with self impatience. What a nonsensical way to go on!

When he had finished his sandwiches he got up, buttoned his overcoat, said good-night to the landlord and left. Conversation would break out as soon as he closed the door.

He cut through one of the narrow, communicating lanes to the city centre, crossed over and walked up Judson Street with the yellow glare fom the Golden Cockerel ahead of him. Riccy Bourg was having his grand reopening.

The club entrance was squeezed between a male boutique and a music shop which had a window full of guitars and electronic gadgetry. The doorman, a pug in a monkey suit which was too small for him, met him just inside the door.

'Are you a member, sir?'

Wycliffe showed his warrant card and followed it with a photograph of Elaine Bennett. 'Have you seen this girl at the club?'

The pug held the photograph at arm's length.

'I seen her a few times.'

'When and who with?'

'She's been coming here off and on for months, a couple of times she was with a young man but most often she's with a party, several men and girls together. That sort turn up lateish, to finish the night off like.'

'There must be scores of girls who come in and out of this place in the run of a week.'

'Hundreds.'

'Then how do you remember this one?'

The pug looked knowing. 'Well she caused trouble, didn't she, and Mr Pirelli, the floor manager, pointed her out to me.'

'What sort of trouble?'

'Well I wasn't there, was I? I mean, I'm down here, but I heard she was drunk and made a scene with Debbie Joyce.'

'Is Mr Bourg in the club?'

The man made a move to the stairs. 'I'll see if he's there, sir.'

'You stay where you are.'

Wycliffe went upstairs and through the swing doors into a foyer where the smell of fresh paint struggled with a drench of commercial perfume. A girl in red, skin-tight pants and the sketch of a bra' asked for his membership number but settled for his warrant card and his coat. As she turned to hang up the coat he saw that she had a golden cockerel embroidered across her bottom; very fetching. What price women's lib?

Another set of swing doors and he was in the main room of the club. Plush lined booths round the walls, a dance floor in the middle and a band on a raised dais at the far end. Subdued lighting and a decor in red and gold. The night was young and there seemed to be more girls in red pants than customers. A young man in a red dinner jacket with a frilly shirt and a hairdo and beard like Disraeli's showed him to a booth and offered him a menu and wine list the size of a newspaper.

'Drinks are served at the tables, meals are available from ten until one. Our hostesses are delighted to partner unaccompanied gentlemen and the cabaret starts at ten. Games of chance in our salon through the curtained doorway by the dais.'

Wycliffe lit his pipe. One of the hostesses, a tall brunette with a sulky expression, came over to him.

'Care to buy me a drink?'

'Sit down.'

He showed her his warrant card. 'Police.'

'Just my luck.'

She was pretty under her make-up but her skin must have been very pale for the lighting only succeeded in making her look pink and naked.

'What's your name?'

'Della—Della Paterson.'

'How long have you worked here?'

'Just over a year.'

'So you knew Debbie Joyce pretty well.'

'I knew her all right.'

'How did you get on with her.'

'She was a bitch. The fact that she's dead won't alter that.'

'Is that your opinion or do the others share it?'

'Nobody liked her, she would do the dirt on anybody.'

'Like the pianist?'

She looked at him, surprised. 'So you've heard about that. He was in good company. I could write a book about her dirty tricks.'

'She seems to have got on with the boss.'

114

The girl nodded. 'He thought she was special. According to him she was what the customers came to see.'

'And was she?'

We shall soon find out, shan't we?'

'Did she sleep with Bourg?'

The question really surprised her. 'With Bourg? You must be joking! He never looks at anybody but his wife. As far as he's concerned we're just part of the furniture. Hey up! Here he is.'

Riccy Bourg had come through the curtains by the dais and was crossing the floor towards Wycliffe all smiles. He signed to the girl and she got up and went.

'Mr Wycliffe!'

'Your people must be slipping, I've been here ten minutes.'

'They jest tell me. I am much pleased to see you but we talk better in my office.'

'We talk better or, at least quicker, here.'

Riccy sighed and took his considerable weight off his feet.

'It's about poor Debbie. Why you come to me I don't know, I tell your young man—'

'It's about this girl, Elaine Bennett.' Wycliffe put Elaine's photograph on the table in front of him. Bourg looked at it with distaste.

'Who is this? She is not working for me.'

'Have you seen her in the club?'

He spread his hands. 'You ask me? Hundreds of girls come through that door. You expect that I remember?'

'This one, yes. Your muscle man remembers her very well.'

'Pouf! He is only bone above the neck that one but I will put on my glasses and look again.'

He produced a spectacle case and took from it a pair of spectacles with the thickest horn rims Wycliffe had ever seen.

'Now, I look'

But at that moment a party of six or eight came into the room. The glasses came off, the band seemed to be rejuvenated, Bourg signalled frantically to the young Disraeli and it was some time before his thoughts returned to the photograph.

'Yes, she has been here. Half a dozen times, maybe more.'

Things were beginning to warm up. Two men came through the swing doors, laughing, saw Wycliffe and went out again.

'There, you see? You are bad for my business sitting there, Mr Wycliffe.'

'So the sooner you tell me what I want to know . . . '

'But I do tell you.'

'Not enough. What was the connection between her and Debbie?'

'Connection? What is this?'

'Something happened between them—here.'

Bourg looked at Wycliffe then at another group which had just arrived. 'It was nothing.'

'Tell me about it.'

Bourg looked at the ceiling. 'She was drunk, the girl in the picture. Six months ago, maybe more. She is in big party, you understand, three, four tables. Much laughing and a little fooling. No harm. There is cabaret and Debbie is singing. When she is finished singing, Debbie visit the tables, talk to the customers, have a little drink with them. They like that and it is good for business. Well, this night she join the table where your girl is with her friends and after a short time there is commotion and I go over to see. Your girl is more drunk than I think so I am very smoothing and I ask her what is wrong. She is very excited and she tell me that Debbie is under false pretences. She is not Debbie but is called Rosaline something.' He smiled broadly. 'Well, this is not news to me. This I know. Debbie Joyce is professional name but I cannot make the drunk girl under-

116

stand this and so I ask her friends to take her home. There is no more trouble.

'Afterwards Debbie say she knew the girl when they was at school.'

'The girl has been back several times since.'

'Of course. Why not? No more trouble. When you are drunk you sometimes get very fixed idea that something is important then, when you are not drunk — pouf! All forgot.'

'You know that this girl has been murdered also?'

A calculating look from the brown eyes. 'I see it in the paper.' He shifted uncomfortably. 'I'm sorry but it has not to do with me.'

'This is a case of double murder, Mr Bourg, it would be very unwise to play games.'

But Wycliffe knew better than to see Bourg's attitude as necessarily sinister. His reflex response to the police was defensive and he was likely to appear most guilty when he had least to hide.

His chat with Bourg seemed to confirm that the only significant contact between the two girls had been while they were at school. But how did they become 'two of the guilty ones' nine years later?

'My men will have to question your staff about what you have told me.'

Bourg shrugged. 'But not tonight, eh? Tonight I get back some of the money I spend on making the place look so good.'

The club was filling and the cabaret started as Wycliffe was leaving. A stand-up comic with an Irish accent and a florid complexion told blue jokes one after the other.

Outside Wycliffe looked round for a bar, he wanted to get the feel and taste of the place out of his system. Tolerant of most things, he had difficulty in finding any common ground with the habitué of places like the Golden Cockerel. Vice in a cellophane wrapper with a red ribbon made him sick.

117

# CHAPTER SIX

Thursday was another fine day but the wind had gone round to the north-east and strengthened, a bitter wind, dry and searching, probing every crack and crevice, stirring the dust in the streets and whipping up white horses in the estuary.

*The News* on Wycliffe's desk bleated triumphantly:

DRAMATIC DEVELOPMENT IN CITY MURDERS
EXCLUSIVE!
'I AM NOT A PSYCHOPATH!'

A photograph of the note was given a three-column spread in the middle of the front page.

More encouraging, W.P.C. Burden had returned from Paignton with a snapshot she had found amongst the mountain of stuff which Elaine's mother had treasured. Three girls of fifteen or sixteen, dressed in jeans and T-shirts, sprawled on a grassy slope in front of a disused hut that was half ruin. In the background, rocky outcrops and a moorland scene.

The girl with the mop of dark curls had been identified by her mother as Elaine, the second was Debbie Joyce, he could not think of her as Rosaline Parkin, less still as Rosaline Norman. The broad, high cheek-bones and the pointed chin were unmistakable.

118

The third girl, fair, plump and smiling was a stranger and somebody must have taken the snap.

Mrs Bennett was unhelpful. 'We never knew any of Elaine's friends. She never confided in us. I don't understand it really . . . we did all we could.'

Mrs Bennett did, however, remember Elaine spending a holiday after her 'O' levels at a hostel in Dorset, but she had not heard of any trouble there.

Wycliffe gave instructions for enlargements of the photograph to be made and for one to be sent to *The News*, others to the regional TV stations.

WHO IS THE THIRD GIRL?
NUMBER THREE—DO YOU KNOW THIS GIRL?
DID YOU TAKE THIS SNAP?

Ready-made headlines and almost certainly the quickest way to get answers.

He telephoned the editor of *The News*.

'Exclusive?'

'Not this time.' All the same it was from the local press that he expected results.

'You are taking over my front page.' Editors feel compelled to grumble even when good copy falls like manna from the skies.

Two girls had been murdered and in the mind of their killer they had been killed as a punishment—*two of the guilty ones.* Presumably there were others. Wycliffe had started from the assumption of a link between the two girls and it seemed logical to suppose that a similar link must exist between the dead girls and others marked down by the killer. If the nature of the link could be firmly established, if the real common denominator could be found then it should be possible to anticipate the killer, to know his intended victims and to protect them. So far it had been shown that Debbie Joyce and Elaine Bennett had known each other when they were schoolgirls and they had since met at Bourg's club. But Wycliffe was not entirely satisfied

119

with Bourg's account of the clash between the two girls. Without some deeper cause of enmity it was unlikely that Rosaline Parkin, merely by changing her name, would provoke such a demonstration from Elaine drunk or sober. He sent for Dixon.

'Della Patterson is a hostess at the Golden Cockerel. I've no idea where she lives but you can find out either from the club or from Bourg. Find her and ask her for her version of why Elaine Bennett and Debbie Joyce were at daggers drawn.'

'You think she'll know, sir?'

'I'll be surprised if she doesn't, she's been at that club for more than a year and I'll bet there isn't much she doesn't know.'

Dixon was on his way out when Wycliffe called him back.

'Are we keeping you busy, Dixon?'

Dixon studied the floor. 'I seem to have plenty to do, sir.'

'Don't you think that might mean that we find you useful?'

Dixon flushed to the roots of his blond curls. 'I hope so, sir. Thank you very much.'

Wycliffe thought of his own apprenticeship when any hint of approval from his superiors would have been interpreted by him and his contemporaries as softening of the brain. Times change.

Gill came in wearing a new suit which would soon acquire the slept-in look which distinguished all his clothes.

'I've had Lincoln C.I.D. on the phone; a chap called Evans—a Taff—says he worked with you when Noah wore rubber drawers.'

'Has he got anything for us?'

Gill sat down. 'Little enough. The Russells have lived in Saxby, near Lincoln, for generations. Dolly's father and mother kept an hotel. She was an only child. They retired some years ago and went to live on the

120

coast but they're both dead now. There are still relatives about but they have no knowledge of or interest in our Dolly. I gather that she was unpopular —stuck up.' Gill paused to light a cheroot which he had been waving about in his hand. 'One of the relatives, a maiden aunt, says she had a letter from Dolly some time ago. It was an odd sort of letter and she ignored it.'

'How do you mean, odd?'

'I gather that it was about money but the old lady can't remember the details. She's going to try to find it but Evans says her house is like the bloody British Museum without a catalogue.'

The connections between the two murdered girls seemed slender enough but Wycliffe felt that it was the line to follow, and if he was right, the school teacher might turn out to be an important source of information. It was certainly more promising than a massive deployment of manpower to offer the public the illusion of security. Such exercises cannot be maintained and they are notoriously ineffective in catching criminals.

All the same he realised that he would have to make some move in that direction and with the co-operation of the uniformed branch and by drafting in men and cars from divisions outside the city he was able to muster a substantial force of mobiles which would patrol the city at night without exhausting his resources too rapidly. The administrative arrangements took him most of the morning and he handed over the operational planning to Gill.

Among the reports which came in was one from Scales. He had interviewed the surgeon, Matthew Norman, who appeared to have been thoroughly co-operative. Norman stated that he had been on an emergency case in the theatre at Millfield from half-past eight until gone eleven on the night Elaine Bennett was murdered. Enquiries at the hospital confirmed that Norman had successfully operated on the victim of a car crash who had suffered extensive abdominal injuries. He had been in the theatre for nearly three hours.

Exit Norman as a suspect in the Elaine Bennett case but Wycliffe had never taken the possibility of his guilt very seriously.

He was completely immersed in the case now, so much so that he was irritated by the intrusion of anything not strictly relevant. Usually he followed the national and international news with closest attention, eight in the morning on the radio, nine at night on the telly, these were sacred hours. But he had not heard a news bulletin for more than twenty-four hours. His responses to the world about him were automatic and disinterested except as they concerned or might concern his case.

Mr Bellings, the deputy chief, telephoned. 'You are an elusive fellow, Charles!'

Wycliffe, never communicative, was almost mute with Bellings.

'I think we can expect trouble from the press, Charles.'

'I don't doubt it.'

'So far they are being kind to you but it won't last . . .'

Bellings did not finish his thought. He had a stock of unfinished sentences which enabled him to make various points without actually saying anything quotable. He was saying now that another killing was almost inevitable and that it would do Wycliffe's reputation a lot of harm and not only in the press. If you listened to Bellings for long you would begin to believe that every time a dip snatched an old-aged pensioner's purse there were political repercussions. Bellings had a complex mind, he and Machiavelli would have understood each other.

'Apart from the preventive measures about which I received your memo, what other steps had you in mind?'

'I thought of writing him a letter.'

'A letter? Through the press?'

'It will have to be, I don't know his address.' He thought that he had gone too far and added, 'Call it an appeal, if you like.'

'But my dear Charles, you might as well appeal to a mad dog not to bite!'

'Perhaps, but it might be worth trying. We need time.'

Bellings took it hard. 'With three separate incidents there must be some leads.'

'There are but they haven't led anywhere. You've seen my reports?'

Why did he do it? Gratuitous provocation? Not really. His approach to his job was personal and immediate, Bellings saw everything in terms of press reaction, political and administrative repercussions, statistics and reports. There was little common ground, no hope of mutual understanding. They rubbed each other the wrong way at every contact but Bellings was able to conceal his feelings more effectively because he had the instincts of a diplomat.

'I think you should put the idea to the chief before you carry it any further.'

'I shall do, if I decide that it's worth doing.'

Was he serious about writing an open letter to the killer? Almost. The idea was growing on him. The man was sensitive to public opinion and it was just possible that such a move might put him off his stroke for a day or two, perhaps long enough to pull him in. It was worth a try. He picked up the telephone to speak to the chief constable but the chief was out of town until lunch time on Friday.

He mooned about his office most of the afternoon. He had arranged for detectives to visit the secondary schools in the city in an effort to discover the name of the girl whose parents had complained about her treatment at Miss Russell's community holiday. A trivial incident nearly ten years old. Was it likely that anyone would remember? His best hope was to find the school teacher herself and he had made it known to the press that the police would be glad to interview her.

Somewhere in the city there was a man who had killed twice and intended to kill again.

Intended was probably not the right word. *Would* kill again, he couldn't stop himself.

Wycliffe knew that there must be times when the man was tortured by doubts; hours or even days when he almost closed his mind to the knowledge of what he had done and so dulled the agony of remorse. Then came resolution, he would stop now. He would never kill again. He would give himself up. If they put him in prison he would be safe. But slowly, inevitably, his resolve was undermined, his conscience spoke to him with a different voice. If he stopped now he would be running away, betraying his trust. Reluctantly he would come to see that he must go on, it was his duty, part of the burden he carried. And so the way was made smooth for his next act. The mechanics of the crime, planning the where, when and how were exciting. He became intoxicated by his capacity for clear, incisive thought and for prompt, decisive action. The tension grew from hour to hour, the rhythm quickened and the climax came.

It was a cycle.

D.C. Dixon reported directly to Wycliffe on his visit to the night club hostess, Della Patterson.

'She has a bed-sitter in a house in Bear Street, sir, down by the old harbour. I got there round one and she'd just got up—'

'Did she tell you anything?'

'In the end. At first she was a bit coy, said she'd already told you all she knew about Debbie Joyce.'

'Well?'

Dixon, obviously pleased with himself, wanted to make the best of his tale.

'It seems that the real trouble between Elaine Bennett

124

and Debbie was over the floor manager, a chap called Pirelli.'

'Mr Disraeli?'

'Sir?'

'Never mind. What about him?'

'Apparently Elaine fell for him in a big way and for several weeks there was quite a thing going between them. Even some talk of marriage.'

'But Debbie put a stop to it?'

Dixon nodded. 'True to form, according to Della Patterson. She made a dead set at Pirelli and when she'd cut out Elaine she dropped him. There was no love lost between Debbie and the other girls, apparently she'd done the same thing before.'

'It's a wicked world, Dixon.'

'Yes, sir.' He lingered. 'A good many people must have felt like killing that girl, sir.'

'Fortunately there's a big gap between feeling like killing and doing it. And who felt like killing Elaine Bennett?'

'That's a more difficult one, sir.'

The telephone rang.

'Huntingdon C.I.D. on the phone for you, sir.'

After the usual preamble he asked, 'Any joy?'

'At first it didn't look very promising. Lady Margaret's is run like a nunnery, all the staff are resident and it's virtually impossible to do any unofficial snooping, but we had a stroke of luck. It turned out that our super has a friend whose daughter was involved in the Russell affair. It was largely from what she and one or two other girls told their parents that Miss Russell was asked to resign. Of course, she did and it was all smoothed over with no nasty scandal.'

'She was a lesbian?'

'So it seems. Is that what you were after?'

'I wanted to know why she resigned.'

Wycliffe asked one or two more questions but learned nothing new.

If this girl had received unwelcome attentions from Miss Russell and told her parents ... But it all happened nearly ten years ago. He kept coming back to that.

It was dark and once more he sat at his desk with only the green-shaded desk lamp to light the big room.

In the end he went home because he could think of nothing else to do.

He drove slowly out of the city and as he got clear of the suburbs he could feel the car being buffeted by the wind.

The living room of their new home had been made by knocking two rooms into one. There was a dining area at one end and they could sit down to a meal while they watched the ceaseless flow of traffic through the narrows at the entrance to the port. Even at night, unless the weather was bad, they often left the curtains undrawn so that they could see the pattern of light-buoys and the slow procession of ships up and down the channel, marked only by the lights they carried.

'Where are they?'

The twins, both of whom were doing post-graduate courses at university, were still on Christmas vacation.

'There's a film on at the Arts they wanted to see.'

'So long as they're together.'

'You're worried about Ruth?'

'I'd just as soon she was with her brother in the evenings until they go back or until we catch this joker.'

'Any prospect of that?'

'Not so's you'd notice.'

'I'll serve. It's fresh prawns with mushrooms and a curried sauce.'

They ate in silence. Wycliffe usually made the coffee but he did not stir and she went instead. When she came back he was sitting in his armchair staring at nothing.

'Coffee?'

He took the cup mechanically. Helen washed up without his help and when she came back he was still sitting. She settled down with a book—*Coastal Gardening*.

'Got a pencil?'

Helen looked up from her book. 'There's a ball-point in the magazine rack.'

'I know, how long since you've used a pencil?'

Helen closed her book on her finger. 'I can't remember, I usually use a ball-point or nylon tip. I think I saw a few pencils in one of the drawers of the cabinet.'

'In other words you don't use pencils and neither do I.'

'Is that something for the *Guinness Book of Records* or does it lead somewhere?'

'Our chap wrote his note to the paper in pencil—very soft—probably 5B.'

'Perhaps he sketches or draws or something.'

'I'd just got round to that.' He got out his pipe and started to fill it. 'Valerie what's-her-name, the girl who was attacked on the allotments, said that he smelt of turpentine.'

'So he paints as well.'

Wycliffe shrugged. 'It's a thought.'

## CHAPTER SEVEN

Sheila Barker née Jukes was getting breakfast for her husband and two children. Clive, aged one year, squatted disconsolately in his play-pen, beating the bars with a plastic toy; Denise, two and a half, lying on the floor, was scraping a crayon over a black and white picture of the Magic Roundabout.

Sheila, who had changed only predictably in nine years, was fatter, her breasts sagged more heavily and her mouth was a little harder and meaner.

Her husband called down the stairs, 'There's no socks in my drawer, Sheila.'

'They're still in the airing cupboard.'

A radio on the side board churned out pop music interspersed with inanities from the duty D.J.

She went into the kitchen and returned with an egg on a spoon which she plopped into an egg cup in her husband's place. 'Your egg's ready.'

The letter box rattled and she went out into the passage, returning with the morning paper. A picture on the front page and the headline above it caught her eye: Did You take this Photograph? Do You know the Third Girl?

When her husband came down she was still looking at the paper, spread out on the table.

'Look at this.'

Barker was swarthy, small and bony, already thinning on top though he was still under thirty.

He glanced at the picture and the headlines. 'They're still at it, then.'

She pointed with a fat, pink forefinger, 'That's Rosaline, that's Elaine Bennett and the fair girl is Joan Simmonds. I wonder what they're after.'

Her husband sat in his place and sliced the top off his egg.

'You'd better tell 'em.'

'Why should I get mixed up in it?'

'No, I wasn't serious. It's got nothing to do with us.'

Sheila folded the paper and put it on the sideboard. 'Funny though.'

'What is?'

'Those two being killed like that. What are they supposed to have done?'

'Done?'

'In that note he wrote to the paper he said that they were the guilty ones.'

Barker laughed shortly. 'You don't want to take any notice of that nonsense. He's kinky—mad as a hatter.' He spoke with his mouth full of bread and egg. 'Just don't go gallivanting round the streets at night.'

'Fat chance I've got doing that. When will I see you again?'

'Not tonight. There's a brief session on the new promotion this afternoon and that means I shall have to stay in Bristol overnight. With luck I should be back lunch time tomorrow.'

Miss Russell and her partner were at breakfast in their high, narrow kitchen on the first floor. Originally it had been a part of a bedroom which had now been partitioned to give a kitchen and bathroom. They ate a Swiss cereal breakfast with milk but no sugar and drank black coffee.

Miss Russell, now forty-eight, had changed little

129

except that her hair was grey and tiny bristles sprouted on her upper lip.

'There's the paper boy, Janet.'

Miss Carter, dumpy and cheerful, waddled downstairs to collect the paper off the mat. She came back up slowly, reading the front page.

'Look at that.'

She dropped the paper by Miss Russell's plate.

DID YOU TAKE THIS PHOTOGRAPH? DO YOU KNOW THE THIRD GIRL?

Miss Russell glanced at the headlines and at the photograph.

'What will they dig up next?'

'Do you know the other girl?'

'Yes, that's Joan Simmonds, they won't find her in a hurry, she's married and living in Malta.'

'Perhaps you should tell the police.'

Miss Russell regarded her companion with scorn. 'Why should I put myself out? It's all nonsense anyway, a newspaper gimmick I shouldn't wonder.'

'Those two girls have been murdered.'

'Probably because they asked for it. That Rosaline Parkin had all the makings of a tart and, from what I saw of her, Elaine Bennett wasn't much better.'

'You saw what the killer wrote to the paper yesterday —about punishing the guilty. He must have meant something.'

'Rubbish! It probably wasn't the killer who wrote it anyway. In any case, what's it got to do with me? I happened to have taught one of the girls, that's all.'

Miss Carter, as always, was bludgeoned into agreement by her companion. 'I suppose you're right. There must be plenty of people who will recognise the girl without you being involved.'

Miss Russell glanced at her watch. 'It's time I went down, the parents will be arriving.'

Friday was a day of frustration. Although Wycliffe was

beginning to feel that he was on the right track and a number of leads were being followed, results were slow to come in. He feared that the third victim would be attacked over the weekend or shortly afterwards and, so far, he was helpless to prevent it.

The photograph of the three girls appeared in the morning paper:

DID YOU TAKE THIS PHOTOGRAPH?
DO YOU KNOW THE THIRD GIRL?

How long would it be before he got answers to these questions? Surely, with two girls already dead the third and whoever took the snap would lose no time in contacting the police. But Wycliffe knew from experience that many people have a surprising capacity for convincing themselves that whatever misfortunes befall others, nothing can happen to them.

But all publicity generates some response and by mid-day several women had been to their local police stations claiming to know the third girl; three, including a matron of fifty claimed to be the girl and two remembered taking the photograph. All were regulars, ready to oblige with a confession or an identification at the drop of a hat.

The Department of Education, prompted by the Home Office, came through with the information that Dorothy Russell, when she resigned from St Margaret's, had cashed her pension contributions and ceased to be a registered teacher.

After lunch Wycliffe saw the chief constable and, despite an objection from Bellings, obtained permission to publish his own letter to the killer. He spent a good deal of the afternoon drafting the letter and, when it had been typed, he sent a copy to the editor of *The News*.

In the early evening he drove idly round the city. It was not that he wanted to check on Gill's dispositions, he did not, in any case, expect that they would serve any useful purpose except to reassure the public. He drove through the streets to keep contact, because he could not work from the abstractions which other people put on paper for his benefit. He passed through the city centre and down Prince's Street. There were few people about and not a lot of traffic. The wind played tricks with the litter in the gutters.

The street lighting was poor and none of the shops was lit. That girl in the light-coloured coat, hurrying along the pavement, her body slanted to the wind, she probably felt safe in one of the main thoroughfares of the city but a resolute killer might do his work and be away before anybody realised what was happening. There would be no safety until he was taken. A police car cruised slowly down the middle traffic lane.

He reached the dock gates and turned off into a maze of streets where terraces of mean little houses alternated with the blank walls of warehouses. As he made his way northward semi-detached villas with front gardens took the place of terraced houses and there were no warehouses. Before the Second World War these had been the outskirts of the city, now the urban sprawl had engulfed former villages in all directions.

The killer was a man of the suburbs, Wycliffe felt sure of that. Once he had been at home in a neatly patterned subtopia where each tiny garden had its forsythia, its flowering cherry, floribunda roses and bedding plants in season. He did not belong to the world of fish-and-chips and betting shops. There were thousands like him but he was different because he was a killer.

The crime cars and panda were geometrically spaced, weaving complex, interlacing patterns through the streets.

The killer was vastly outnumbered but he had the choice of time and place. He could say to himself at any time when the odds seemed weighted against him, 'Not tonight.'

Or could he?

Was it not more likely that each time the resolution to kill needed time to grow, time to mature and that when it had he would be driven irresistibly to act.

Wycliffe sighed. A family man without a family. The phrase came to him out of the blue and he savoured it. It expressed two paradoxical ideas which had been in his mind for some time. The killer, a family man who knew what it was to have ties and obligations, responsibilities and compelling loyalties—'People cannot destroy lives without being punished'. And the killer, a lonely man, haunted by ghosts.

But the paradox went deeper than that. From the beginning he had insisted that the man was rational to the extent that he did not kill at random; his victims were 'the guilty ones'. This had practical importance, it offered some prospect of discovering the killer through establishing his motives which was the reason for laying such emphasis on links between the victims. On the other hand Wycliffe, without splitting psychiatric hairs, was prepared to maintain that any multiple killer is mad, in particular that a multiple strangler cannot be sane. But, in his view, there was no necessary contradiction in attributing rationality to a mad man.

If he was right the crunch might come later, when the killer had run out of victims; that is to say when he had killed 'the guilty ones'. Then his madness might become irrational or, at least, require a further process of rationalisation.

At nine o'clock he made for home. The wind brought with it occasional flurries of sleet which clogged the screen-wipers. Helen saw that he was tired and dispirited and asked no questions. He allowed himself to be fussed over, dry sherry in front of the fire followed by a light meal. Fillets of sole poached in white wine with shrimps.

'Sole dieppoise,' Helen explained. 'I couldn't get any mussels so I used shrimps instead.'

Helen's cooking was much influenced by their last trip abroad. One year he had endured sauerkraut and sausages.

On the ten o'clock news they screened the picture of the three girls with the police appeal for information.

At eleven they went to bed but lay awake until after midnight listening for the twins to come in.

Prince's Street was the only one of the city's main throughfares to have escaped both the blitz and the developers. It was still a street of small shops interspersed with pubs, and many of the proprietors still lived in the rooms over their shops. The street had remained unchanged for long enough to attract the attention of conservationists and it was becoming increasingly the vogue to speak of it as 'interesting' rather than seedy.

One shop which was both interesting and seedy had changed little in fifty years. The signboard read: Probert and Rendell. Artists' Colourmen. Picture Framers and Restorers. In the shop window there was a large, gilt-framed oil-painting. It depicted a sea scene with fishing boats in the middle distance and a crowded jetty in the foreground. Exactly one half of the picture was encrusted with dirt and varnish so that the design was scarcely discernible while the other half was so clear and bright that the colours might have been just applied. Apart from the painting there were two display racks in the window showing a range of mouldings and a card which stated: Estimates free.

Jim Rendell worked in what had once been a conservatory, built on to the back of the house. His partner and former employer, now seventy-five, looked after the shop but left most of the mounting and framing and all the restoration work to him. Anyone who judged their prosperity by the number of customers coming to the shop would have been misled for they were regularly employed by collectors, galleries and even museums throughout the south.

The glass walls of the conservatory had been replaced by brick but the sloping glass roof remained. The room had been divided by a partition and in one half Rendell did the restoration and mounting while in the other he had his picture framer's bench, his tools and stocks of mouldings. A cast-iron stove with a rusty smoke-pipe heated the whole place more or less effectively except in the coldest weather. The smells of turpentine, paint and glue were blended with the slightly sickly odour of linseed oil. An alarm clock, ticking away on top of a roll-topped desk, showed half-past five.

Rendell set about making a parcel of six small watercolours which he had mounted and framed in Hogarth moulding. He worked as he always did, systematically and without haste, completely absorbed in his task. As he was tying the string Alfred Probert came in and stood in the doorway. He was short and on the stout side. Long white hair and a moustache gave him a superficial resemblance to Lloyd George which he had cultivated, believing that there had never been a real statesman since the little Welsh wizard. He took a silver watch from his waistcoat pocket and compared it with the alarm clock.

'You off then, lad?'

'I'm off.'

'Are those Mr Walton's watercolours?'

'Yes, I'll leave them in the shop, he's calling for them in the morning.'

'What's up then, won't you be here in the morning?'

'It's Saturday.'

For fifteen years Rendell had not come to work on Saturdays but each week the old man pretended to be surprised.

'Well, I'll go upstairs to my tea. Mrs Probert doesn't like to be kept waiting. You'll shut the shop? Turn the lights out and lock up?'

135

'Yes. Good-night.'

'Good-night, lad.'

The same ritual every night, almost the same words but he never felt impatient, he would not have had it otherwise. He had worked with Probert for thirty-nine years, first as his apprentice, then as an employee, and for the past fifteen years as a partner.

He took off the long grey overall which he wore over his suit, hung it on a nail by the door and put on his mackintosh and cap. A quick look round the two rooms and he switched the lights out. Light came through faintly from the shop. A short passage and he was behind the counter in the shop where there was nothing displayed for sale. He switched out the light, let himself out through the shop door and locked it behind him, trying the door twice before he was satisfied.

A cutting wind blew down Prince's Street and he turned up the collar of his mackintosh. The shops were poorly lit, the street lamps were meagre and lorries thundered down the broad thoroughfare on their way to and from the docks. He waited his chance, then crossed in two spurts. It was not far to the *Guardian* building.

As usual, in the city centre, he waited until he was within a few feet of the newspaper seller before he allowed himself to read the placard.

MYSTERY OF THE THIRD GIRL

He had seen the paper that morning so he knew what they were talking about. The photograph had had a strange effect on him. He had not known of its existence, there was no reason why he should have done, but the fact that the police had found and published it made him feel insecure. It was like an attack from behind, it made him realise that things were going on of which he had no knowledge.

136

He bought a paper.

The newspaper man said, 'Joining the big spenders, guv?'

He walked slowly past one of the big stores, reading in the light from the windows.

The photograph appeared for the second time under the caption: THE MYSTERY GIRL and the text went on to say that up to the time of going to press no one had come forward to identify the third girl in the picture nor had the police heard from whoever took the photograph.

> If you recognise the girl or if you know anything of the circumstances in which this photograph was taken you are urged to telephone police headquarters, Telephone 323232, or get in touch with any police station.
>
> Long-standing Vendetta?
>
> The importance attached to this photograph by the police suggests that they take seriously the note which the killer addressed to this newspaper and which appeared in our columns yesterday . . .

His hands trembled so much that he could not continue to read. He folded the newspaper and walked on slowly, breathing deeply to restore his calm.

'Is that you, Jim?'

He changed his jacket and came slowly into the living room. Albert was there.

'What you buy a paper for? You know we always get one.'

'Don't go running off, Jim, I'm just dishing up.'

If only they would leave him alone!

\*    \*    \*

In the morning, by the time they had finished breakfast, the estuary was lit by the almost level rays of the sun, emphasising the contours of the landscape through highlights and deep shadows. A Norwegian vessel, her decks stacked with timber, crept up channel against the tide; a tug, towing a train of barges made out to sea. Wycliffe stood in the window of the living room and smoked his first pipe of the day. Soon now the killer would be opening his newspaper and he would read the famous letter. But would he telephone?

'I expect that I shall be in the office all day.'

'What about tomorrow?'

'I don't know. It depends. I could have incoming calls on the special number transferred to me.'

His son, David, had left the old banger which he shared with his sister across the garage entrance. It was going to be one of those days.

He drove into the city and parked his car in the space which had his name painted on it. MR WYCLIFFE. Next to him was MR BELLINGS and next again, MR OLDROYD, the chief constable. Two other spaces were labelled; the hoi-polloi below the rank of chief superintendent had to fend for themselves. Bellings' E-type Jag was in his space but the chief's Rover was not. The chief believed that one of the privileges of rank should be a free weekend.

Wycliffe was morose, not because anything had gone wrong, not even because the case was bogged down but because he felt ineffectual and useless. All he could do was sit at the end of a telephone and wait.

At eleven o'clock he received a call purporting to come from the strangler. 'About your letter . . . '

There followed a description of what the caller proposed to do with his remaining victims. The details were obscene as well as impracticable. Telephone engineers and police were monitoring all calls to the special number and within a very short time, after dropping the receiver, a call came through on another line.

'A call-box in East Street, sir. There were two cars

138

within easy reach so they should have him by now. What do you want done with him?'

Wycliffe considered. With these chaps, fortunately, it was all in the mind. 'Tell him if we catch him again we'll do him and let him go.'

Gill came looking as though he hadn't slept. 'We seem to be getting nowhere fast.'

They had lunch of a sort sent up from the canteen.

At a quarter to two, after three more calls from kinks who claimed to be the strangler and while they were drinking a second cup of coffee, a call came through from St Thomas's Road Police Station.

'Inspector Rigg, sir. There's a young lady here who says she's got information about the photograph published in yesterday's papers.'

'Genuine?'

The inspector was careful. 'I think so, sir. She's certainly about the right age to have been at school with the girls. She seems a sensible sort . . . '

'I'll send a car to pick her up.' He signalled to Gill who had been listening on the second earpiece. Gill gave instructions over the intercom. Within twenty minutes she was in Wycliffe's office.

'Barlow—Pamela Barlow née O'Brien.'

Red-gold hair to the shoulders, green eyes and, of course, freckles. A broad forehead and a firm chin. She wore a yellow raincoat and neat little square-toed shoes with wedge heels. Good legs. A dish—an Irish dish. She certainly earned Gill's approval.

'I live at twenty-three Water Lane, not far from St Thomas's Station.'

She had a copy of The News of the previous day on her lap with her handbag.

'They say you want to know about the third girl and who took the snap.'

Wycliffe nodded. 'That's right.'

'Well, I took the snap and the third girl was called Joan Simmonds.' She smiled. 'At least that was her

139

name before she was married, she's called Roberts now; her husband is in the R.A.F. and they're stationed in Malta.'

'You're sure of that?'

'Of course. I had a letter from her Thursday.'

'Where was the photograph taken?'

'On the moor. It was a Saturday and the four of us were on some sort of charity walk. I can't remember the details.' She pulled her skirt over her knees. 'I know we stopped in front of that disused army hut to have our lunch.'

'Charity walks don't sound to me like Rosaline Parkin's cup of tea.' Gill was being frighteningly amiable.

She laughed. 'Well, she didn't finish the course. When we reached the road she hitched a lift back.'

'She was a friend of yours?'

'Not really. She was Elaine's friend. I went about with Joan Simmonds and Joan was friendly with Elaine. That's how it came about. In fact we went about quite a bit together at that time.' She fiddled with her handbag. 'Actually Rosaline and to a lesser extent, Elaine, had a reputation for being a bit wild and good girls were supposed to keep away.'

'And you were a good girl?'

'Mother thought so.'

Wycliffe intervened. 'Joan, Rosaline and you were all at the same school—at Cholsey Grammar, is that right?'

'Yes. Elaine was a cut above us, she went to Bishop Fuller's. She and Rosaline and Joan Simmonds met playing hockey. I was no hockey player but all four of us used to meet some weekends.'

Gill stared at the girl. Wycliffe stared at his blotter. Winter sunshine streamed in through the window. Traffic was building up on the road outside. A fine Saturday afternoon and half the population wanted to get out of the city.

'We shan't keep you long, Mrs Barlow.'

'Don't mind me, my husband is glued to the telly on Saturday afternoons.'

'Being at Cholsey Grammar, you would remember Miss Russell?'

'Oh, yes, I remember her well enough.'

'I understand that she used to organise various vacation trips. Did you go on any of these?'

She looked surprised. 'I went on two, one was a camping holiday, the other we spent three weeks in a hostel.' She smiled again. 'An exercise in communal living, she called it. It was that all right.'

'Elaine Bennett and Rosaline Parkin went on both?'

'No, neither of them was on the camping trip.' She looked at Wyclife with a puzzled frown. 'What is all this?'

Wycliffe ignored her question. 'How many girls altogether were at the hostel?'

She thought. 'Twenty-four or five, I suppose. Most of them were from Cholsey Grammar but several other schools were represented.'

'And Miss Russell was in charge?'

'Oh, yes. She was the only teacher. She organised it.'

'Did anything happen during those three weeks— anything you might think of as disturbing or even alarming?'

She pursed her lips and frowned. 'I think I know what you're after but why, I can't imagine.'

'What are we after?'

'The fuss there was about that girl.'

'What girl?'

'I can't even remember her name, she wasn't one of ours.'

'You mean that she came from another school?'

'She must have done but I can't remember which. She wasn't in the same dormitory as Joan and me, she was in with Rosaline and Elaine.'

'Tell us what happened.'

141

For the first time she hesitated. 'I wish I knew what this is in aid of. All the same, if you want the gory details ... It wouldn't mean anything unless you know that Miss Russell was a les. At least ...'

'At least what?'

'Well, it's difficult. I mean, she liked to paw some of the girls, I don't think anything very bad happened.'

'Were you one of the girls?'

Curse of red hair and freckles, she blushed. 'Yes, I didn't like it but there wasn't much you could do. I mean, she made out she was being specially nice to you. Perhaps she was in her own way.'

'Rosaline too?'

'Rosaline especially. She got really browned off with the treatment.'

'What happened?'

She was reluctant. 'It really was quite nasty when you come to look back at it. I only heard the details when it was over. Of course, Rosaline was behind it.'

The two men waited.

'This girl that all the trouble was about was a real innocent and in the dormitory with that lot she had a good deal to put up with. One of her fads was that she didn't like taking a shower with the other girls so she used to get up early before the others were about. Of course, Rosaline got hold of this. She and Elaine and a girl called Sheila Jukes worked it all out. While this girl was in the shower they pinched her dressing gown and pyjamas so that all the poor kid had was a towel. She stuck it out in the showers for a while but in the end she had to come out. She made for the dormitory but they'd locked the door. Then, along comes Rosaline and pretends to be sorry for playing the joke on her. She said, "Your things are in Miss Russell's room, all you've got to do is go in and get them."

'By this time the kid was nearly in tears and she said she couldn't go into Miss Russell's room with no clothes on but Rosaline told her not to be a fool. How did she think they'd got the stuff in there if the Russell was still in bed? She'd gone to the staff bathroom and everybody knew she took ages.

'Of course it was all lies but the kid believed her and opened the door of Miss Russell's room. As she did so Rosaline called to her, she turned to answer and Rosaline took a photo—a flash photo.'

Gill grinned with unusual ferocity. 'What a pleasant little crowd! What happened?'

'Not much at first, then, a few days later, prints of Rosaline's photo appeared on the notice boards and all over the place. There was this girl with nothing on coming out of Miss Russell's room. The door, by the way, had Miss Russell's name on it.' She stopped speaking, fished in her bag and came out with a packet of cigarettes. 'Do you mind if I smoke?'

Gill lit her cigarette.

'After that I'm not entirely sure what happened. I do know that the poor kid who was the victim of it all was sent home in disgrace. Joan Simmonds and I had to go with her in a taxi to the station to make sure she got on the train. She was in a terrible state.' She drew deeply on her cigarette and exhaled with obvious pleasure. 'Nothing happened to Rosaline and the other two as far as I know. The rumour went round that Rosaline had warned Miss Russell that if she made any fuss the headmaster would get to hear one or two things. Anyway, it all seemed to die a natural death and it wasn't long afterwards that Miss Russell left to go to another school.'

Wycliffe had made one or two cryptic notes in the convolutions of an elaborate doodle.

'This Sheila Jukes you mentioned. Was she from Cholsey Grammar?'

'Oh, yes, she was another of Rosaline's cronies.'

'You haven't kept in touch with her?'

She leaned forward to tap off the ash from her cigarette. 'No, we never had much to do with each other and I haven't heard of her since she left. She left in the lower sixth and I went on to "A" levels.' She sat back in her chair with a half smile on her lips. 'Now, do you mind telling me why you wanted to hear all this?'

Wycliffe still offered no explanation. 'We are anxious to get in touch with Miss Russell.'

'Well, that shouldn't be difficult. I saw her last week.'

'Here—in town?'

'In the central market. I spoke to her but she pretended not to see me—she was always good at not seeing people if she didn't want to.'

'You're sure it was her?'

'Positive—and she knew me, I could tell. She turned away that bit too quickly and became absorbed in a baby-wear stall.'

Wycliffe was looking at her with expressionless eyes. 'Didn't it strike you as odd that both victims of the killer should have been girls who were involved in this rather sick joke?'

She frowned. 'No, I can't say that it did, it only struck me how horrible it was that they should be two girls I knew.' She hesitated, then went on, 'You can't really think that there is any connection, surely? I mean, it would be too ridiculous, wouldn't it? After nine years!'

Wycliffe's face was still blank and his manner unusually pedantic. 'We are on the look-out for any links between the two murdered girls and you have told us of one such link, there may be others.'

'I see.' She looked doubtful and a little worried.

'Now, about this Sheila Jukes . . .'

But Pamela Barlow had told them all she knew. As she was leaving she turned to Wycliffe, the green eyes full of concern. 'You don't think it's possible . . . I mean, if he's mad . . . after all, I did come here, didn't I?'

Wycliffe was reassuring. 'I am sure you have no cause for worry, Mrs Barlow, but I will see that your house is kept under observation especially at night.'

When she had gone, Gill slumped back in his chair and

lit a cheroot. 'I agree with her, it's bloody silly. All this for some damn fool kid's prank which happened nearly ten years ago.'

Wycliffe looked at him without speaking. Gill had never seen him so sombre. His manner was almost menacing. 'At least you know what you have to do.'

A little later he stood by while Gill briefed his men for the search. 'Dorothy Russell, aged 48, and Sheila Jukes, aged 25 . . .'

When Gill had finished he turned to Wycliffe out of courtesy. 'Anything you'd like to add, sir?'

Wycliffe looked startled, as though his thoughts had been elsewhere. He snapped, 'Just find them while they're still alive.'

For the next couple of hours he haunted the control room where radio links with all the cars were maintained. From time to time the officer on duty was prompted to speak to him, to make some casual remark but Wycliffe behaved as though he had not heard.

Scales was the first to report back. 'Sheila Jukes used to live at fourteen Stokes Road, Cholsey. It's a council housing estate. Her father was—is for all I know, a welder. I got that from the headmaster at Cholsey Comprehensive and I'm on my way there now. Sergeant Ellis is gone to Harcourt Mansions, a block of flats where Miss Russell lived when she was at school. It's our only starting point.'

Stokes Road was a long, depressing string of semi-detached council houses built between the wars. Each had its little front garden bounded by concrete posts and wire mesh. There was a light in number fourteen and Scales could hear the television. A teenaged girl answered the door and looked him up and down with interest. 'Jukes? There's nobody here called that. Mam! There's a man here asking for somebody called Jukes.' She was joined by a thin, middle-aged woman with permed and dyed hair, eye-shadow and a cigarette which seemed glued to her bottom lip so that it bobbed up and down as she spoke.

'Jukes? They've been gone ages. love. Emigrated. We moved in here when they went.' She considered. 'Five year ago last August.'

'Emigrated?'

She eyed him speculatively. 'Australia, I think it was. He was a welder; good trade for emigrating, they say. You a relative?'

'Police.' He produced his warrant card. 'We wanted to get in touch with their daughter, Shelia.'

'Oh, Shelia—that's different. She didn't go.' She massaged her bare arms against the cold. 'She married some fella just before they left and she stayed behind.'

'Do you happen to remember her married name?'

'No, dear, sorry. We wasn't what you might call friends. It was just when we first come to see about curtains and things they was getting ready for this wedding.'

'Was it a church affair?'

'Oh, yes, with all the trimmings. St Andrews, over across the railway.'

Scales thanked her and raised his hat.

'She's done something?'

'Oh, no. Just a routine enquiry.'

St Andrews was the parish church of what had once been the village of Cholsey. It had retained its grave-yard intact with its avenue of yews and the vicarage had kept its garden but housing development pressed in on all sides. Scales reported in on his car radio.

The short drive up to the vicarage was muddy and unlit. A lighted window to the right of the front door was the only sign of life and his ring was answered by the vicar himself, a tall, spare man with fringes of grey hair, bald on top.

'Do come in!' He was taken into the room in which he had seen the light. A large room with a dusty decorated ceiling and oak panelling half way up the walls. There elegance ended and gave place to tattiness. A thread-

146

bare carpet, deal bookshelves, a cheap plastic shade where there should have been a chandelier, an ancient gas fire standing in a grate made for logs. The vicar's desk was littered with books and papers. 'I was working. You must forgive the muddle. A detective, you say, I would have taken you for a bank manager or a solicitor.' The vicar meant to be complimentary.

'You were asking about the marriage of someone called Jukes?'

'The bride was Shelia Jukes, the marriage took place about five and a half years ago and we want to know her married name.'

The vicar dangled a pair of heavy library glasses and regarded Scales with a knowing smile, 'Barker—she is now Mrs Shelia Barker.'

'You have a good memory, sir.'

'On the contrary, I have very bad memory. It happens that you are the second person to come to me with that question.'

Scale felt his spine tingling.

'Three weeks, perhaps a month ago—certainly before Christmas, a gentleman came to me with the same enquiry. He said that he was an old friend of the family and that he had lost touch. He had been told that they had emigrated but that Shelia had married and was living in the city. Like you, he wanted to know her married name so that he could find her.' The vicar paused, reasonably, for breath. 'I searched the Registers, and, of course, there it was—Jukes/Barker.' A benign smile.

'This man, could you describe him?'

'My visitor?'

Scales nodded.

'Oh, dear, this does sound ominous! I saw little enough of him. He arrived, like you, out of the night one might say. It was bitter cold and raining; he was muffled up with an overcoat and scarf. He refused to some into the house so we went straight to the vestry

147

where our parish records are kept in a safe. A very few minutes while I searched and he was off again. To do him justice, he donated two pounds to church funds.'

'Old or young?'

'A subjective question, Mr Scales. He was grey and though he was not as thin on top as I, it seemed to me that we were much or an age—fifty to fifty-five.'

'Tall? Short? Thin? Fat?'

'About my build.'

'How did he strike you? Educated? Well off?'

'Oh, dear! These are difficult questions! I would say that he could have been a superior type of workman, a tradesman with his own business, perhaps.' Momentarily the vicar saw himself in 222B Baker Street, he was pleased with himself.

'Think, if you will, sir—was there anything about him—his manner, his dress, his speech, his appearance which struck you?'

The vicar reflected. 'No, I can't say that there was. He seemed to me to be a pleasant man in a little too much of a hurry to be quite as polite as he would otherwise have been. He might, even, have been nervous.'

They went to the vestry by a muddy path still littered with rotting beech leaves. Their way was lit by the vicar's flashlight. The vestry was damp and badly lit. It was a feat of strength to open the door of the massive old safe. The records showed that Sheila June Jukes had married William Edward Barker on the 3rd July.

Wycliffe's restless prowling brought him to the radio room just as Scales' second report was coming in. He was cheered, it was progress. With any luck it would be simple to locate Sheila Jukes and they had another witness who had almost certainly seen and talked with the strangler. It might be possible to get out some sort of identikit picture but Wycliffe had little faith in that prospect. Most people do not have the kind of visual memory which is necessary.

Wycliffe went through the Voters' List. There were

three William Edward Barkers and one of them was listed with Sheila June Barker at 3 Parkes Road, Maudsley. Maudsley was the nearest of the eastern suburbs, only a short distance beyond Godolphin Road. He looked them up and found them in the telephone directory.

He dialled the number. A man's voice answered.

'Mr Barker . . . ? The husband of Mrs Sheila Barker?' Agreement tinged with nervousness and suspicion. 'Detective Chief Superintendent Wycliffe. I would like to talk to you and your wife . . . This evening . . . Thank you. In fifteen mintes.'

He drove out to Maudsley, along Godolphin Road, past the allotments. Although it was a fine evening there were few people about. Maudsley is a maze of roads which happened between the wars, some of them are still unsurfaced and unadopted and peter out unexpectedly into waste ground. Parkes Road was a crescent of semi-detached villas, the road lined with cars. His ring at number three was answered at once. A young man, swarthy, dark, already balding, the sort one expects to sell something. He received Wycliffe with a blend of nervousness and aggression. The sitting room was littered with children's toys. Barker waved him to a seat.

'The wife will be down in a minute. What's it all about?'

Wycliffe refused to be drawn until she arrived. She was blonde, pink and plump, running to loose fat, her eyes protruded slightly and she had a small, rather mean mouth. She looked at Wycliffe, 'Well? What are we supposed to have done?'

Wycliffe was bland. 'Nothing! Nothing at all. I want to ask you one or two questions and from what you tell me I shall know whether you need our help or not.'

She frowned. 'Why should we need your help?' And her husband demanded, 'What's all this about? We've got a right to know.'

149

'Did you, Mrs Barker, once know a girl called Rosaline Parkin?'

She nodded. 'I went to school with her.'

'And Elaine Bennett?'

'I didn't go to school with her.'

'But you knew her?'

'What if I did?'

'You will know that they have both been murdered.'

She looked at her husband and back to Wycliffe. 'What's that got to do with us?'

'Have you had anything to do with either of these girls since you left school, Mrs Barker?'

'No, I haven't, and anybody who says different is a liar!'

'Nobody does. The point is that we want to find out the link between the two girls—the reason why the killer chose them; then, knowing the link we might be able to make a shrewd guess at his next victim.'

They spoke together. 'Are you saying . . .?'

'Just that we have found only one real link between the two girls and that you were involved in that link.'

Barker got out his cigarettes and offered one to Wycliffe who refused. His wife's manner had undergone a complete change. 'Are you suggesting that I . . .?'

Wycliffe would not let her finish. 'I've no idea but we can't afford to take risks.'

'But the man is mad, he kills anybody . . .'

'We think not.'

Barker blew out a thin ribbon of smoke. 'You mean that Sheila and these two girls . . . but it's bloody fantastic! You heard her say yourself she hasn't had anything to do with them since she left school.'

'It's just possible that these crimes have their origin in events which took place then.'

Barker looked incredulous but his wife was worried. 'Give us a fag, Ted.' Her husband gave her a cigarette and lit it for her.

150

Wycliffe went on. 'You will remember a holiday with a party of girls in a youth hostel. You, Elaine Bennett and Rosaline Parkin played a cruel prank on one of the party . . . .'

'I don't know about cruel, the kid was a creep, still wet behind the ears.'

'So you remember the incident?'

She smiled a little nervously. 'Yes, I remember it all right, it was a bit of a giggle.'

'I want to know the name of the girl who was your victim.'

'Look here, if my wife is in danger we want protection.'

Wycliffe was chilling. 'Your wife will be best protected if we catch the killer. Now, Mrs Barker, about this girl . . .'

She shook her head. 'I don't know her name. I don't think I ever heard it. We used to call her Buttercup which got shortened to Butters. She wasn't one of our lot.'

'What school did she come from?'

Mrs Barker looked surprised by the question. 'How should I know? She wasn't from Cholsey, I know that.'

'What was she like?'

'I told you, a dyed-in-the-wool little creep.'

'In appearance?'

'Oh, mousey—straight hair, cut fairly short; plain with freckles. Not very tall and thin—skinny.'

'Did she have any friends?'

'I shouldn't think so.' She paused. 'Wait a minute, there was a girl, another of the same sort—Buttercup and Daisy we used to call them. I haven't a clue what she was really called either.'

'Or the school she came from?'

'No, I'm sorry. It was the first polite word she had spoken.

Try as he would he could get no further and he turned, reluctantly to the question of protection.

151

'Are you at home each night, Mr Barker?'

'No, I'm away two or three nights a week, I'm a rep for E.C.A. detergents.'

He arranged for a police officer to be in the house day and night and for Mrs Barker to be accompanied whenever she went out.

'No, I don't go out much. The chance would be a fine thing. With two kids under school age and no car when Ted is away . . . '

Barker came to the gate with him. 'You seem to think this is pretty serious.'

Wycliffe was cool. 'Two girls have been murdered.'

'I hope there won't be any balls-up over this. If anything happens to my wife . . . '

'If anything happens to your wife, Mr Barker, I shall be most disturbed.'

He had telephoned instructions over the Barkers' phone and he waited by his car until he saw a patrol car turn into Parkes Road, then he drove back to headquarters.

The streets were quiet, the crime cars and pandas conspicuous.

Three girls had played a sadistic prank on a fourth nine years ago. A school teacher, for reasons of her own, had seemed to connive in their cruelty. Two of the girls had been murdered, one was now under police protection, that left the teacher.

Nothing new at headquarters. He decided to go home.

# CHAPTER EIGHT

On Saturday morning he took his bed linen and his underclothes to the launderette. Alice would have washed them for him, gladly, but he would not allow that degree of intimacy. He bought a paper and looked with trepidation at the headlines. He received another shock:

### AN OPEN LETTER TO THE KILLER
Detective Chief Superintendent Wycliffe, Head of Area C.I.D., writes to the killer of Debbie Joyce and Elaine Bennett through the columns of *The News* ...

He could scarcely believe his eyes. He stepped into a goods entrance out of the press of Saturday morning shoppers, so that he could read without being jostled.

Detective Chief Superintendent Wycliffe, Head of Area Crime Squad, writes to the killer of Debbie Joyce and of Elaine Bennett through the column of *The News*:

'I read your letter to the newspaper and I accept your word that you are not an indiscriminate killer. I believe you when you say that you do not want to terrorise innocent people. But that is what you are

153

doing. Each night thousands of girls and women are afraid to stir out of doors because of you. Two girls have died at your hand and another has suffered injury and shock because, you say, you made a mistake. You seemed to have been upset by your mistake for you telephoned the hospital to ask about her. But how does it feel to have taken the two other lives? How will it feel if and when you murder others? You say that they are guilty, but who are you to judge? Guilt is decided by the processes of law. Are you so arrogant as to believe yourself above the law? If you are not indeed a monster you must have doubts about what you have done and even graver doubts about what you intend to do. Think again. Talk to someone. If you wish to talk to me you can do so by telephoning, day or night, 323232.

> Charles Wycliffe,
> Detective Chief Superintendent.'

What were they doing to him? On top of the photographs of the three girls this was too much.

'You all right, mate?'

He was standing there, staring at the newspaper, while a vanman carrying a huge cardboard box tried to get past. He slipped the newspaper into the bag with his washing and rejoined the endless stream of shoppers.

After he had washed and rough dried his clothes he went to the market and bought flowers. In the afternoon he would catch a bus to Colebrook cemetery and put his flowers on the grave. All this had become routine over the past few months, his Saturday routine. Until tea time he could pass the day well enough going about the tasks he had set himself with a sense of purpose. But this letter . . . He thrust it resolutely to the back of his mind; it would be evening before he had to face its real challenge. Most evenings Albert and Alice were busy about their offices and he had the flat to himself. He read. An avid and undiscriminating reader, he went to the library twice a week and read whatever he happened to pick up there. But on Saturday evenings Albert was free and there was no place in the flat where he could read in peace. Even if he retreated into his bedroom it was not long before Albert would open the door—'Mind if I come in? I was thinking . . . '

So, after his first Saturday night in the flat he had gone out. He had wandered aimlessly around the city streets with the feeling that he was excluded from every human activity. In his wanderings he chanced on a little bar in Chester Street, between a Chinese restaurant and a bookmaker's. It was quiet there, he could sit in a corner and watch the regulars. In particular he watched four men who were there every Saturday playing solo. By listening to their conversation and without exchanging a word he had come to know a lot about them, their work and their families. It would have been the easiest thing in the world to have become involved and the possibility frightened him though he could not have said why. Whenever one or other of the card players caught his eye he frowned and looked away.

On this particular Saturday evening, between hands, they chatted about the strangler and speculated as to whether he would try again and if he did whether he would be caught.

The manager of the shoe shop, a little pot-bellied man, was dogmatic. 'It's obvious, he's a nutter. He'll go on until they catch him. That sort won't be put off. I mean, you or I would reason out our chances . . . '

The builder who, except when he was in the act of drinking, had a pipe between his teeth, shook his head knowingly. 'They never caught Jack the Ripper, did they?' He waited to let his point sink in. 'I mean, I agree with you, he's a mad man—he must be, but that doesn't mean he's stupid. They're cunning. I've got a cousin who used to work in Broadmoor and the things he told

155

me you wouldn't believe! Like I said—cunning.'

He was not disturbed by their conversation. He listened avidly and was strongly tempted to join in. It gave him a feeling of confidence and superiority to hear their absurd comments. But he wanted to say, 'It isn't like that! You haven't the least idea . . . '

The giant with a red face who was a wholesale grocer was dealing another hand and the conversation petered out as they picked up their cards.

'What's trumps?' The fourth man looked like a prize-fighter but he was a foreman for the council.

'Clubs.'

'I'll try a solo.'

'Abundance on hearts,' from the builder.

'Pass.'

The manager of the shoe shop studied his cards. 'I'll try a mizzy.'

They played in silence and the manager made his call.

'If I had my way I'd bring back hanging. Mad or sane, they think twice if they know they're going to get the same as they dish out.'

The grocer blew out his flushed cheek and belched. 'Hanging's too good for the likes of this one. I mean, it's obvious, they don't actually say so in the papers but you can read between the lines, he's after only one thing and he's ready to kill for it. Bastard ought to be castrated!' He laughed. 'Make the punishment fit the crime, that's what they say, isn't it?' He turned toward the solitary stranger who had sat watching their play for several Saturdays. 'I can see that you agree with me, sir. Castrate the bugger!'

He felt himself trembling. 'The girls were not raped!' he spoke the words in a voice scarcely above a whisper but he saw the attention of the four men suddenly focused on him. He got up, leaving more than half his beer in the glass, and walked out.

In the street he was still trembling and his heart was

racing. He walked quickly as though he were trying to shake off all connection with the episode, as though he could leave it behind. His thoughts raced with his heart but they made little sense. He found himself muttering over and over again, 'You're a fool! You're a fool!' It was a fine evening and there were plenty of people about, twice he collided with someone and walked on with no apology.

By the time he was once more aware of his surroundings he had reached Prince's Street. Prince's Street, dimly lit, most of the shops shuttered and dark and despite the heavy traffic the pavements were like shadowy lanes except where the pubs made an orange splash of light. Now that he could think more clearly, he was afraid, afraid of the consequences of what he had done but more of the lack of control which made it possible for him to do it. What had he said? 'The girls were not raped!' And despite what the grocer had said several papers had stated that there had been no sexual assault. It was not so much what he had said as the way he had said it. And as though to dramatise the thing, to underline it, he had walked out.

'Hullo, darling.'

He stopped, confused, too absorbed in himself to realise at once what was happening.

'Hullo, darling. Want to come home?'

She was standing in a passage by the newsagent's, her thin, pale features lit by a street lamp. Then he understood and walked on. He heard her bored, indifferent voice, 'Suit yourself!'

He was tempted to turn back. Why not? He needed something to relieve the tension which had built up until it threatened his safety. It was tension—not wholly fear—but half-pleasurable excitement which kept the nerve endings tingling and seemed to cut him off from his surroundings. It was dangerous, if he had had any doubt of that this evening's episode had dispelled it. He turned, but she was already talking to another man.

Just as well.

He decided that he would go back to the flat. He would have his supper and by that time he could reasonably go to bed.

Albert was watching Match of the Day with a plate of sandwiches and a glass of beer on the table beside him. Alice was ironing.

'You're back early.'

'I thought I'd have an early night.'

'Good idea. There's some sandwiches; shall I get you a can of beer from the fridge?'

'No thanks, I'll just have a sandwich.'

He went to bed but it was a very long time before he got to sleep. He had kept the morning paper and he re-read the letter. He had been hurt and angered by what the newspapers had written about him and he had tried to explain. He had written to them, the anonymous thousands who read the newspapers and believe what they read. He wanted to put the record straight and he genuinely wanted to reassure people who were unnecessarily afraid. The last thing he had expected was a reply. Now it seemed almost as though he had addressed his letter to one man. He could not explain how he felt, even to himself, but this stranger, this policeman, had taken advantage to steal into his private world and to question what was already settled.

He turned off the bedside lamp and lay, staring at the ceiling. It was never dark in this room; at whatever time of night he woke he could see across it, the handbasin, the mirror gleaming, and his green-handled tooth-brush. It was never silent either. Although the street below was usually quiet after midnight the main road through to the docks was less than a quarter of a mile away and the distant rumble of traffic seemed endless.

For a long time he turned and tossed in his bed. Once he got out and remade it. At all costs he had to avoid thinking about the future. Afterwards. Through most of his life he had taken a childish pleasure in looking forward to things, small things. An outing, doing a special job about the house or garden, holidays ... Several times, especially during the past day or two, he had had to struggle to extinguish the doubts which troubled him, but he had been able to fight it down.

Now ...

He felt that he was on the verge of being cheated, perhaps of cheating himself. After all the labour he had put into his plan. It had not been easy, he had traced four people who had been involved in an event which had occurred nine years ago. Four women, three of whom had since changed their names. He had gone about the task with patience and dogged persistence and he had succeeded. Now, half his plan was accomplished.

He told himself that it was too late for doubts, he had cut himself off with no place in the world for any other person. When Rosaline Parkin died he had ended the possibility of life for himself. 'There is no going back!' He found himself saying the words aloud through clenched teeth. Strange! At the start it had all seemed so straightforward and necessary.

He heard the church clock of St George's strike three on its cracked bell. Even after that it seemed that he did not entirely lose consciousness.

On Sunday morning he woke well before it was light, as on any other morning. Rather than disturb the others by moving round he read in bed until he heard Albert stirring. Albert for sure, Alice liked her bed, especially in the mornings. He joined Albert in the kitchen and they made coffee. It was the one time of day when his brother-in-law was taciturn so he did not have to talk. The day dawned fine and cold with clear skies. From the flat he could look out over the city and glimpse the sea, remote, pure and sparkling in the morning light. At nine Alice came in wearing her dressing gown with her hair in curlers. She made breakfast.

Although she was his sister, Alice irritated and

repelled him. She was fourteen years younger so that they had not shared their childhood. She was blonde, plump and pink skinned; secretly he thought her gross. And she offended his sense of decency when, as now, she went round the flat wearing only her dressing gown which often failed to hide her heavy breasts. He compared her with his Rose who had been slim and dark and pale.

'What's the matter, Jim? You look peaky. Doesn't he, Albert?'

'I'm all right.'

'I don't suppose you'll be in for lunch?'

'No, I think I'll go over to the house.'

'Why not stay and have a decent meal for once?'

'No, I think I'll go over, there are several things I want to do.'

She shrugged. 'It's no use arguing with you but you don't look well.'

It had been the same with small variations on each of the Sundays he had been at the flat. Each Sunday he had reached the city centre in time to catch the 622 bus at ten o'clock. He was building a new habit pattern which would soon be as inflexible and necessary to him as the one it had replaced. But how long could it last?

The streets were almost deserted and they looked shabby and unkempt in the sunlight with the litter of Saturday still lying about in the gutters and on the pavements. He went up to the top deck of the bus.

He avoided looking out of the window while the bus was in Godolphin Road. After Godolphin Road the suburban sprawl thinned for a time then congealed again into a spider's web pattern of semi-detached houses and bungalows centred on the one-time village of Maudsley. Beyond Maudsley a dreary industrial estate, then Crowley; more urbanised countryside with the mushrooming university buildings, then Rhynton. Twenty-seven years ago when he bought his house in

Rhynton it had been cheap, now there was competition to live that far out of the city.

He got off the bus by the pub and turned up Oakshott Avenue. Most of the houses in the avenue had garages and several of the men were out washing their cars on the concrete aprons. They greeted him with what seemed excessive friendliness as though they were anxious to make up for something.

Number thirty-seven was a corner house on the junction between Holland Drive and the avenue. The wooden palings were neat and well soaked with creosote and the privet hedge above them had been geometrically clipped. The windows shone and the curtains were drawn by just the right amount proclaiming that there was nothing to hide but no desire to display. He went to the front door, inserted his key, opened the door and passed inside. 'It's only me!' The house was silent but the shining black and white tiles in the hall, the well hoovered carpet on the stairs and the gleaming white paintwork all spoke of a well-cared-for home from which the housewife had popped out to the shops or, perhaps, to church.

He picked up a couple of circulars from the mat and went through to the kitchen, opened the back door and collected a pint of milk from the step. He was experiencing an odd sense of detachment, an unreal calm. He seemed to be wholly absorbed in what he was doing, leaving no room for other thoughts, yet on the very fringe of his consciousness he was dimly aware of emotional conflict, of tension and turmoil. But it seemed at the moment to have little or nothing to do with him.

He got dusters and a vacuum cleaner from the cupboard under the stairs and went upstairs to the back bedroom. He opened the casement window and let in the cold, fresh air. Then he started to dust.

It was a single room with a divan bed. The bed was covered with a blue, linen bedspread and lying on it

161

was a pyjama case in the shape of a dog with 'Jane' embroidered across it. There was a bedside cupboard, a built-in dressing table, a chest of drawers and bookshelves, all painted white with gilt fittings. He had made them all himself in those long summer evenings and during weekends which now seemed dream-like in recollection. Everywhere he looked he was reminded of years which had been the happiest of his life. One of the walls was almost covered with pictures of Jane, beginning with her as a baby and ending with the same photograph as he had on his chest of drawers in the flat, the girl with short, straight hair. She looked sixteen or seventeen.

'The three of us'—that had been the phrase constantly on their lips. From the beginning Jane had been a participating member of the trio, loved, protected and involved. His daily work had been no more than a necessary interruption of their lives at home. He worked hard because he wanted to secure the best for the three of them. Since his marriage to Rose no voice had ever been raised in anger in their house.

But he and Rose had seen the danger of overprotectiveness too late.

He finished his dusting and started to vacuum the carpet. It was then that he seemed to reach a decision. He switched off the machine and went downstairs to the telephone in the hall. He did not need to look up the number. He picked up the receiver and started to dial then he remembered that telephone calls can be traced or he thought they could, he wasn't sure. Almost certainly the policeman who had written that letter would have his calls monitored—that was the word. He hesitated, then decided to go to a call-box. He noticed that his heart was thumping and he was trembling a little which must mean that he was excited though he didn't feel it. He put on his jacket which he had taken off to do his housework and let himself out by the front door.

There was a kiosk at the end of Holland Drive but it was too public so he cut through by a footpath to the post office which had one in a sort of yard at the back. Being Sunday, the place was deserted. He dialled 323232. He had no idea what he would say. The ringing tone, the double burr-burr repeated itself four times then there was a click as someone lifted the receiver.

'Mr Wycliffe speaking.'

A pleasant voice, kindly, he thought. His mind was racing but he could think of nothing to say. The silence lengthened and he would have dropped the receiver but the man spoke again.

'I think you must be the man who wrote to the newspaper.'

'Yes.'

'You have something you want to say to me?'

'I think so.'

'Perhaps you would like to come and see me?'

'Yes. When shall I come?'

'When you like, now if you wish.'

'This afternoon. Where?'

'At my headquarters in Morton Road, or anywhere else you prefer.'

'Out of doors. Edgcumbe Park, by the fountain.'

'When?'

'Two clock.'

'You will come?'

'I think so.'

The policeman was beginning to say something else but he dropped the receiver.

As he walked back to the house he still felt detached. It was difficult to believe that what he had just done or what he might do could really affect him.

When he arrived back at the house the boy had delivered his Sunday newspaper. It was lying on the mat. The same paper that he had taken for twenty-five years. In the beginning it had been sober, middle-of-the-road, but over the years circulation chasing had

163

turned it into a careful blend of sex, sensationalism and sentimentality.

LETTER TO A MURDERER!
POLICE CHIEF WRITES TO STRANGLER!

In an unprecedented and highly controversial letter, published in a local newspaper, Detective Superintendent Wycliffe, Head of C.I.D., invites the killer to come and talk things over!

The letter was reproduced in small type and followed by another explosion of king-size black print:

WHAT WE THINK.

We have grown accustomed to do-gooders, egg-heads and kinks who want us to believe that violence can be met by cosy chats on the trick-cyclist's couch but this is the first time we have come across a policeman who agrees with them!

Here we have a killer, a sadistic murderer who is guilty of two vicious killings and who *plans* more. What does our chief of police have to say to this man? We quote:

'I BELIEVE YOU WHEN YOU SAY THAT YOU DO NOT WANT TO TERRORISE INNOCENT PEOPLE . . .'

Laughable? But will you laugh if it is your wife or your daughter who is number three? Not so funny, is it?

WHAT WE SAY .

The scorn, the indignation and the moralising occupied the whole of the front page and spilled over into the nearest thing the paper had to an editorial.

He stood just inside the door, reading, then he climbed the stairs and made for the smaller of the two front bedrooms, the one over the hall. His 'glory hole' they used to call it. A table, a couple of chairs, an easel

164

and a Victorian couch. On the table a jam-jar full of brushes and a box of oil-colours. On the walls, several paintings, views of the city in flat colour. In between the paintings there were framed reproductions of drawings by Michelangelo, Dürer and Leonardo. And there were shelves jammed with books.

He sat on the couch, staring at the floor between his feet. He could no longer understand his own changes of mood and they worried him. There were periods when his feelings seemed to be anaesthetised and for long spells he could go calmly about his affairs unaware, or at least insensitive to the mental conflicts and tensions which sometimes loomed so large that they threatened to overwhelm him. There were other times, brief intervals, when he was elated, when he had no doubts and his whole being was stirred to a strange excitement. Finally there were the dark times when he was weighed down by depression and doubt, when he seemed to have lost any context for his life, when there seemed to be no standards left against which he could measure his conduct or his desires. Lately these moods had succeeded each other more rapidly and with less apparent reason. But he refused to ask himself the question which lingered obstinately in the recesses of his mind.

He was vaguely aware of someone ringing the door-bell downstairs but he did nothing about it and eventually they went away.

He took his wallet from his pocket and from it he extracted a postcard photograph of a score or more girls on a beach, an older woman in the middle. Two of the girls had been ringed. A girl in the middle of the front row carried a card with 'Weymouth—1965' on it. He looked at the photograph for a long time then he got up and crossed the room to the window. The room was cold. Outside the sun shone with a brittle, frosty brilliance. Couples with children were setting out on their Sunday walks; through the centre of Rhynton and

down the avenue to the river. On any fine Sunday afternoon in winter the path by the river was like a parade,
prams, children, dogs.

There were shelduck, mallard and curlews out on the
mudflats and solemn, tweedy men and women watched
them through binoculars. He seemed to feel again a
little warm hand in his.

He must have stayed in the room for a long time but
when it was getting dusk he went down to the hall and
dialled a number.

'Miss Coleman? Miss Dorothy Coleman? ... I'm
sorry to trouble you on a Sunday evening but I understand that you run a nursery school—a school for girls
... Yes, that is what I was told. It is for my grandchild,
she is four ... My daughter is a widow and she is
coming to live in the city ... She has asked me to make
the arrangements ... There are certain things I would
rather not discuss on the telephone ... I'm afraid that
I'm working all day ... If you could see me this
evening ... At seven-thirty ... Yes, I understand ...
My name? Oh, yes, of course—Grant—Douglas Grant.'

His hands were trembling as he replaced the
receiver.

# CHAPTER NINE

Wycliffe was up early for a Sunday, before it was light. He made coffee and took it into the living room to stand by the window and watch the daybreak. The contours of the hills across the estuary slowly defined themselves, the navigation lights in the channel seemed to fade. A cold, steely grey light imperceptibly and slowly changed into a radiance which flooded the landscape with colour. He could not see the actual sunrise because his house faced south-west.

He lit his first pipe of the day.

From his early days in the force, on night duty, he had enjoyed the dawn. He liked to think of people waking from sleep, returning to the world, re-establishing their identities; remembering. But each day for some there would be a sad, perhaps a terrible awakening. You have to take up where you left off. No good fairy comes in the night to spin straw into gold or dreams into reality.

Somewhere in the city the murderer must wake this Sunday morning. Would he know a few moments of innocence before memory came flooding back?

Four schoolgirls and a wicked, perverted joke seemed to have started a train of events which had cost the lives of two of them almost ten years later. Was it possible?

The evidence seemed now to point that way and, intuitively, he was convinced but it was difficult to rationalise the idea. There were three questions: What was the connection between the killer and the schoolgirls? Why did he feel justified in murder? And why nearly ten years late?

There was no doubt in Wycliffe's mind that the killer was a middle-aged man. A husband? More likely a father. He remembered that there had been a complaint from the girl's parents. But why wait ten years? It was easy to say that the man was deranged but there had to be some powerful and continuing stimulus to keep the hatred alive for that length of time and then to kill because of it.

A man with a sixteen year old daughter, an only child, doted upon, over-protected. (Perhaps a little private school—a thought there.) Then, too late, she is encouraged to 'mix'—it happens often enough. The girl does her best to adapt, tries too hard and grows more depressed with every failure. Culminating in the traumatic experience of the wretched Parkin girl's sick joke. Could this have brought about or precipitated a mental collapse? Unlikely.

But even if it did, why wait ten years to do something about it? Perhaps a slow disintegration, the man forced to watch his child gradually losing her identity in a relentless process of decline. He might feel compelled to blame someone for such a blow of fate. Rightly or wrongly (truth seldom counts in such matters) he might trace the origin of his grief back to some single incident, clearly, explicitly defined.

As an idea it was thin, but it was possible. He decided to do two things, he would get a list of the girls of the right age who had died in the city during the past year and he would get another list prepared of girls who had been admitted to mental institutions in the same period.

Taffy Evans, now Superintendent Evans, chose to

telephone Wycliffe at his home rather than talk to headquarters. After recalling incidents which Wycliffe had forgotten and in the face of unrelenting taciturnity, he came to the point.

'I spoke to your man, Gill ... Oh, so he told you—you're lucky, boyo, my blokes tell me nothing ... About the Russell woman, her aunt found the letter, bless her woolly vest! She was asking her aunt to put up money for a scheme to start a prep school for girls. She had a premises in view, a country house outside Hereford. She said that she had the capital her parents left her but that she needed another seven or eight thousand. Auntie didn't want to know so she didn't bother to reply.'

Wycliffe asked if the letter was dated and from what address it had been written.

'It's ancient history, boyo, 28th December 1970 and it's on hotel notepaper—Brock's Private Hotel, Market Lane, Hereford. I don't suppose she's still there but it's the best I can do for you.'

Wycliffe detested being addressed as 'boyo' and his manner was rather more curt than the circumstances merited.

But the information was of little use.

Although a police appeal had gone out on the radio and on television there had been no response from Miss Russell. If Pamela Barlow really had seen her in the city market her silence must surely be deliberate. It was understandable that if she had re-established herself in the city she might want to avoid opening old wounds but it was just possible that the killer had reached her already. A woman living alone might not be missed for some time.

He heard the door open. His daughter, Ruth, in her dressing gown. Ruth was getting to grips with herself as a woman, leaving behind the gaucherie of adolescence.

'What's the matter? Uneasy conscience?'

She grinned. 'I smelt coffee.'

They sat on either side of the electric fire, drinking coffee in cosy silence.

Afterwards he telephoned his headquarters to get them moving on his two lists—registrations of deaths and admissions to mental homes. Not that they were likely to get far on a Sunday.

The newspapers arrived and he leafed through them. On the whole, a restrained and sympathetic press. One had chosen him as this week's burnt offering. But he was too hard bitten to be bothered by it. Bellings would be agitated.

At half-past eleven the telephone rang. He was in the living room alone. Helen and Ruth were in the kitchen getting lunch, David was still in bed.

'Mr Wycliffe speaking.'

The silence told him that this was the call he had waited for.

'I think you must be the man who wrote to the newspaper.' Mustn't try to hurry him, on the other hand don't give him too long for second thoughts.

'Yes.'

'You have something you want to say to me?'

Hesitation, painful and prolonged. 'I think so.'

'Perhaps you would like to come to see me?'

The door of the living room, opened and David came in, wearing his dressing gown, dishevelled from bed. Wycliffe held up a warning finger.

'Sorry!'

'Yes. When shall I come?' The voice had increasing assurance.

'Whenever you like—now if you wish.'

'This afternoon—where?'

'At my headquarters in Morton Road, or anywhere else you prefer.'

More hesitation. 'Out of doors. Edgcumbe Park, by the fountain. Two o'clock.'

'You will come?'

'I think so.'

'You . . . ' The receiver clicked back on to its rest and Wycliffe's phone buzzed. He replaced his receiver. A brief interval than another ring.

'Wycliffe.'

'He was calling from Rhynton, sir; a box behind the post office. A call has gone out to all mobiles in the area.'

Rhynton. Subtopia with a vengeance. The tall, thin man would now be hurrying home through the suburban roads, back to his semi-detached. A fine Sunday morning, people who knew him were bound to see him but they would never suspect. A solid citizen.

At noon headquarters called to say that they had missed him. The first mobile had arrived at the post office within three minutes of the message from the monitors but too late.

It came as no surprise to Wycliffe, he had not counted on such an easy win.

'Who is in this morning?'

'Mr Gill is in his office, sir.'

'Put me through . . . Jimmy?'

Gill was sour. 'So they've balled it up.'

'You heard what he said to me?'

'I got them to play me the tape. Do you want me to put men in the park.

Wycliffe hesitated. 'One good man who knows how to keep out of where he's not wanted.' He stopped to light his pipe with the receiver wedged against his shoulder. 'We shall have to do a house-to-house in Rhynton. Get it organised, Jimmy.'

'You think he'll come?'

'I wouldn't bet on it.'

They sat down to lunch at half-past twelve. A light meal. Helen was inflexibly opposed to the traditional Sunday lunch which lays out its victims until three. The sun was shining on the water and streaming into their living room. But for the skeletal elms on the hill opposite it could have been summer.

'I thought I might work in the garden for an hour,'

Helen said. 'Are you going out?'

He nodded. With the university term looming the twins had decided to stay in and work.

Edgcumbe Park is a typical urban green space, shut off from the encircling roads by a thin belt of trees. Swings and slides for the kids, a pond with a fountain, slatted seats, wire litter baskets and lavatories tucked away behind rustic trellis next to the potting sheds.

Wycliffe arrived shortly before half-past two and sat on a seat by the pond. Even in the sun it was chilly. There were few people about, two or three children playing listlessly on the swings and half a dozen dog-walkers. There was no sign of a policeman, which was as it should be. He neither expected the killer nor did he not expect him. The man would have seen the letter the previous morning. He had taken twenty-four hours to mull it over, to have second thoughts and second second-thoughts. Small things would influence his final decision one way or another and the fact that he had screwed himself up to the point of telephoning did not mean that he would keep the appointment. He seemed to realise that himself—'I think so' was the best he could manage and Wycliffe believed that he was being entirely honest.

A distinguished looking man in a well-cut overcoat and wearing an Enoch Powell hat advanced purposefully across the turf. A military bearing and a thick, greying moustache. Momentarily Wycliffe thought that the man was making for him but then a middle-aged lady tacked into his field of view, a lady in furs and wearing a floral toque. An assignation. They met on the gravelled path two or three yards from where Wycliffe was seated and without words but by gentle smiles and muted bird-like cooing noises showed their pleasure in the meeting.

Wycliffe waited for an hour then gave up. He found Gill's detective, told him to stay around for a little longer and to radio in if he saw anyone who might be

172

the killer. Wycliffe walked the half mile back to his headquarters through streets which were in the firm grip of Sunday afternoon melancholy. He went to his office and was joined by Gill. Already the light was failing and he switched on his desk lamp.

'No luck, sir?' The grin on Gill's face was unmistakable.

'No, and you?'

'Not so's you'd notice. What's all this about registrations of deaths and admissions to mental hospitals?'

Wycliffe told him.

At four o'clock one of his lists arrived, sent by some clerk to the Hospital Management Committee who had given up part of his Sunday to make it. Three girls between 24 and 26 years old had been admitted to the city's mental hospital during the previous year. Only one was still there and it was expected that she would be discharged soon. Wycliffe telephoned the medical superintendent at his home and after a sticky five minutes satisfied himself that none of the girls was of interest to him.

A little later he had a call from the superintendent registrar. They had met at a civic dinner and the registrar, whose favourite reading was detective fiction, was falling over himself to be helpful. Four girls of about the right age, had died during the year. One had been killed in a car smash, one had died in childbirth. The third girl, who had died of leukaemia was a newcomer to the city. Only the fourth girl looked at all promising from Wycliffe's point of view; she had died of an inoperable brain tumour. She was unmarried. Wycliffe telephoned the police station nearest her parents' home and asked them to get particulars, discreetly.

He sat doodling on his blotter. This girl, the girl who seemed to have been the unwitting cause of all the trouble, must have had a mother but so far he had thought only of the father. Was it likely that the man

173

who committed these crimes returned home afterwards to a wife? A family man without a family—his own words. So what had happened to the wife? He had postulated some traumatic experience which had turned the man's mind and he had assumed that it had been connected with his daughter's mental breakdown or death but the final blow might equally have been a tragedy affecting his wife.

His office oppressed him, he was deadened by it, muffled. He walked along the corridor to a room at the back of the building where Sergeant Bourne, surrounded by paper and filing cabinets, looked after reports and collation for the squad. Wycliffe picked up a file labelled 'Rhynton—House to House' and leafed through it.

'The file is incomplete, sir. They are still at it. The queries are starred in the top right corner.' Bourne was only twenty-five, up and coming. He believed in team work and the divinity of the computer so there was nothing to stop him.

The starred queries referred to houses where the men had not been able to talk to anyone or where the information given was regarded as either unsatisfactory or in some other way significant.

R6 '25 Horton Drive. Householder: George Bray. 35/40. No reply. Neighbour states that the family visit relatives on Sundays.

R21 '14 Coulston Road. Householder: John Harris. 25/30. No reply. Neighbour states that Mrs Harris is in hospital having a baby. Husband is staying with parents for the time being.

R29 '9 Stacey's Road. Householder: James Higgins. 45/50. No reply. Neighbour states that the family always go out in their car on fine Sundays . . . '

A desperate lot of criminals there.

Wycliffe went back to his desk, lit a pipe and started to go through the reports, starred and unstarred alike.

Occasionally he put one aside and ended up with four, all of them starred:

R58 '32 Hyde Avenue. Householder: Simon Kent 50/55. Widower. Lives with unmarried daughter who is now in London staying with friends. States that he spent whole morning in greenhouse.

R79 '6 Farley Close. Householder: Arnold Pearce. 40/45. Married but lives alone. Guarded when questioned about his wife. States that he spent the morning doing his chores and did not go out.

R104 '37 Oakshott Avenue. Householder: James Rendell. 50/55. No reply. Neighbour states that Rendell recently lost his wife and is living temporarily with relatives.

R146 '14 Holland Drive. Householder: Frederick Polski. 50/55. Widower. Married daughter and her husband share house. Polski states that he went for a long walk between ten and lunchtime. Daughter confirms that this is his habit. Married couple spent morning about the house.'

Three widowers and one man who seems reluctant to account for his wife.

Wycliffe looked at his clock, its gilded pointers stuck out from the panelling, sweeping their silent orbits over gilded cyphers. He liked a clock which ticked, with Roman numerals and fretted hands. Seven o'clock. He telephoned his wife not to expect him.

He was depressed and uneasy.

It was a fortnight since the first murder, almost a week since the second. He felt that the next, if there was to be a next, was due—perhaps overdue. Rosaline Parkin and Elaine Bennett were dead; Sheila Barker was under the strictest surveillance which might mean that they had reached stalemate unless the school teacher was on the killer's list. If she was she must be in imminent danger. After having second thoughts about giving himself up the killer might feel a compulsive need to assert himself once more, perhaps even to atone for his moment of weakness.

Wycliffe rang through to Sergeant Bourne. 'Any further reports?'

'D.C. James has just come in with another batch, sir, and two checks on previous interviews.'

'Which?'

A moment's delay. 'R79 and R104, sir, Pearce and Rendell. Pearce was cagey about his wife and the reason seems to be that she's recently left him. She was twenty years younger and she's gone off with another man. Rendell's wife died six months ago and he is now living with his married sister, a Mrs Martin. She and her husband are caretakers of the *Guardian* building in the city centre; they have a flat on the top floor.'

'Has he been contacted there?'

'No, sir, he was out when D.C. James telephoned.

'What did his wife die of?'

Hesitation. 'The report doesn't say, sir, if it's important I'll find . . . '

'Don't bother.'

He lit his pipe and wandered over to the windows. The curtains had not been drawn and he could see the brightly-lit main road with its endless stream of traffic. The windows were misted over by fine rain which refracted the light and distorted the view. He felt helpless.

If the school teacher had been living in the city for six months she should be in the Voters' List but she was not there under her own name. He returned to his desk and picked up the exchange telephone. 'I want to speak to Mr or Mrs Martin, they are caretakers of the *Guardian* building and they live on the premises.'

An interval. 'You're through, sir.'

A woman's voice.

'Mrs Martin?' He was amiable, casual. 'Is your brother there?'

'You've just missed him; he came in and went out again.'

'Never mind. As you know, we are making a routine check on all the occupiers of houses in the Rhynton district of the city . . .'

She sounded helpful, unflustered.

'I understand that your brother has made his home with you temporarily—since the death of his wife . . . Yes, I'm sure it would be. How long has he been with you? . . . Since the beginning of July. Did she have a long illness?'

'She took her own life.'

'I'm sorry.'

'It was very sad.' She sounded a nice woman, genuinely upset. 'Tragic really, they lost their only child, a girl, a few years back and she never got over it. Never the same afterwards.'

'Have you any idea where your brother might be or when he's likely to be back?'

'He went out for a drink, he said he was meeting a friend.'

'Which pub does he use?'

'He doesn't have a regular pub, he's not much of a drinker.'

'It doesn't matter.'

'Shall I tell him to ring you when he gets back?'

'No, don't bother, it doesn't matter.' He thanked her and rang off.

This was it. No dramatic revelations, no blinding intuitive flash, no brilliant deductive reasoning, just the result of plodding routine enquiries. The great detective has it handed to him on a plate by a small army of foot-sloggers who go about ringing doorbells like soap salesmen. Of course, he could still be wrong but he knew that he wasn't.

He telephoned Gill and arranged for a man to be put in the flat and for the house in Oakshott Avenue to be watched. 'The sister will have to be told and we shall want a full description for circulation, photograph if possible.'

Back to the school teacher. It was disturbing that she had not been found and it seemed fairly certain that she could not be living in the city under her own name. If her professional career had ended under a cloud she might well want the past forgotten. In his experience women were singularly unimaginative in the use of an alias. A married woman usually went back to her maiden name, a single woman would often as not chose her mother's. It was worth a try. Without much enthusiasm he put through a call to Superintendent Evans at his home number and sat smoking while he waited for it to come through.

'Her mother's name? I don't have to find out, boyo, I know. Her mother was a Coleman, well known local family, farmers in a big way of business.'

And there she was in the telephone directory, or so he told himself. Miss Dorothy Coleman, The Nursery School, 6 Poulton Avenue. A woman running a nursery school would probably be obsessively concerned to avoid any breath of scandal.

He rang the duty room and told them to send a car to the school, to obtain admission if possible and to wait until he arrived. Then he collected his car from the park and drove to Poulton Avenue. It was a quarter past eight. Fine, misty rain cut down visibility and there were few people about.

Poulton Avenue consisted of large, semi-detached houses built before the first war. A neat little sign on the gate of number six showed up in the light of a street lamp: Poulton Avenue Nursery School.

A police car was parked a little way down the road, the house was in darkness and as Wycliffe drew into the curb a constable came towards him.

'Nobody home, sir. At least, I can get no answer.'

'I'll stay here, you go round the back and see if there's any sign of life there.'

Wycliffe sat in the car. The rain was so fine that it was little more than mist. The street lamps were blurred and the branches of trees overhanging from the gardens formed vague silhouettes, more like shadows.

Footsteps sounded clearly on the flagstones of the pavement and a woman, small and dumpy, stopped by the gate of number six. She looked at the car uncertainly then opened the gate. Wycliffe got out.

'Miss Coleman?'

'Is there something wrong? Who are you?'

Wycliffe introduced himself and she seemed irritated rather than surprised or concerned.

'Why are you here?'

'Perhaps we could talk inside.'

The constable returned and Wycliffe told him to wait. The woman unlocked the front door with a Yale key and switched on the hall light.

'I'm not Miss Coleman, my name is Carter—Miss Carter, I share the house and help with the school.'

The hall was bare and institutional but the stairs were carpeted and she led the way up.

'We live on the first floor.'

'Miss Coleman is not at home?'

'No, as you see, I've just come in myself but Miss Coleman usually goes out for her stroll at about this time.'

'In the rain?'

She smiled. 'It would take more than a drop of rain to put her off.'

He was taken into the front room on the first floor. It was a large room, sitting room and office combined. Old-fashioned chairs with worn upholstery, glass-fronted book-cases, a roll-topped desk with a telephone on it and gilt-framed oil paintings on the walls. Wycliffe was uneasy, partly because he was unsure of his ground. He had only flimsy reasons for supposing that Dorothy Coleman was Dorothy Russell.

'Is Miss Coleman likely to be long?'

'I shouldn't think so, she usually walks round a couple of blocks.'

179

She waved him to one of the easy chairs and perched herself on the edge of another, showing a lot of fat thigh above her stockings.

'How long have you known Miss Coleman?'

'Several years.'

'More than ten years?'

'Probably. Why do you ask?' Her manner was aggressive.

'Did you know her when she was Dorothy Russell?'

She dug in. 'Until you tell me why you are asking these questions I don't propose to answer any more.'

Wycliffe was bland. 'That's reasonable, I'll explain. I think that the woman who was Dorothy Russell may be in very great danger.'

She looked at him as though trying to read his mind. 'You really mean that?'

'I do.'

She seemed to relax her guard. 'I told her but she wouldn't take any notice. She's very obstinate.' She went to a side table and took a cigarette from the box. 'Smoke?'

But Wycliffe had crossed to the desk and picked up the telephone. He dialled and was answered almost at once. 'Wycliffe. I want all mobiles in Number 4 District to patrol roads within a half mile radius of Poulton Avenue. They are to look out for Miss Dorothy Coleman. Late forties . . .' He turned to Miss Carter. 'Height?'

'Five feet five.'

'Build?'

'Very thin.'

'Dressed?'

A moment of hesitation. 'Brown mackintosh with gilt buttons over a maroon trouser suit. She would be carrying an umbrella.'

He repeated the information into the telephone. 'She is to be brought here, to her home at 6 Poulton Avenue. Keep me informed at this number—347489.'

Miss Carter's aggression had disappeared, now she

180

looked scared. 'You really think . . . ?'

'Frankly, I've no idea but we mustn't take chances.'

Taffy Evans had said that the Russell parents had kept an hotel and the furniture here looked as though it had been rescued from the auctioneer's hammer when they sold up. A grandfather clock with a brass face, which must have come from the foyer, showed half-past eight.

'Miss Coleman knew that the police wanted to get in touch with her?'

'Oh yes, she saw it in the newspaper.'

'But she did nothing about it.'

'No, she thought it was all rather foolish.'

'The deaths of two young women?'

Miss Carter was anything but aggressive now; she flushed. 'I didn't mean that! Dot—Miss Coleman thought it was foolish to imagine that what happened to the girls had anything to do with her or with when they were schoolgirls.'

'She didn't want to get involved.'

'No, I suppose not. She can be very obstinate, as I said.' She ground out a half-smoked cigarette in the ashtray.

'What time did you go out this evening?'

'Just before six. I always go to see my mother on Sunday evenings.'

'Is everything as usual?'

She looked puzzled. 'I think so. Dot is often out when I get back.' Her expression changed suddenly. 'I've just remembered something! She had an appointment—not that it makes any difference.'

'An appointment?'

'A man phoned while we were having tea, he wanted to see the school and arrange for his granddaughter to come.' She went over to the desk and turned the pages of a desk diary. 'Here you are, Dot made a note of it—Mr Douglas Grant, seven-thirty.'

# CHAPTER TEN

He had not eaten since breakfast and he was hungry and cold. He must force himself to behave normally or he would do something stupid as he had last night in the pub. Above all he must occupy his mind so that he would not think about what lay before him. This was a trick he had learned in childhood. When a school examination or a visit to the dentist was imminent he would lose himself in a book and when the moment of crisis came it would take him almost by surprise.

While he was upstairs he shut the windows, which he had opened to air the house, then he went downstairs, locked the back door, put on his overcoat and let himself out at the front. He walked down Oakshott Avenue with an easy stride, he looked calm and collected, he *was* calm. There were lights in most of the sitting rooms in the avenue and some had left their curtains undrawn so that he had glimpses of families gathered round television sets. He went to the bus stop in the centre of Rhynton. Another man was waiting there.

'Evening, Mr Rendell.'

'Good evening, Mr Oates.' He thought that his voice sounded quite normal. Oates had lived in Holland Drive for almost as long as he had lived in Oakshott

Avenue and the two men had been acquainted for twenty-five years.

'Been taking a look at the house?'

'Got to keep an eye on things.'

'I suppose you'll be thinking to sell.'

'I haven't thought anything yet.'

He must have sounded brusque for Oates was quick to apologise.

'None of my business, of course!'

An awkward silence before Oates added, changing the subject, 'I suppose you've had the police?'

'The police?' He felt suddenly cold inside.

'Haven't they been to you? They've been going around asking questions. Something to do with the strangler; they seem to think he might live out here.'

'Out here?' He was at a loss what to say.

The bus arrived and they got on together. Oates took a ticket to the city centre and he did the same. It carried him beyond his true destination but he could walk back.

'Shocking business, killing young women.'

'Shocking.'

'Too lax in the courts, that's more than half the trouble. They've got to take a strong line on violence. You look at some of the sentences—you'd think they wanted to encourage it.'

He peered through the window into the darkness.

'I haven't seen you to speak of since your wife ... Very sad, terrible for you. I was saying to Marge only this morning, you've had more than your share ... more than your share.' Oates looked away, vaguely embarrassed by his own words.

He continued to stare at the dimly reflective window. Nothing was required of him but his mind was a ferment.

'I suppose you're still with your sister?'

'For the moment—for the moment.'

They arrived at the city centre and got off together.

'Like a drink before you go in?'

'Thanks all the same but they will be expecting me.'

'Another time.'

'Yes.' He watched Oates as they separated and saw him turn into a bar then he walked in the opposite direction. The police. Why should they think of Rhynton? The telephone call, it must have been a trap. He was shocked, partly because he had nearly made the call from his home, partly because he felt that it was unfair. The feeling of insecurity was almost overwhelming.

His appointment was for seven-thirty but it was now scarcely six o'clock. He felt a little weak and faint, partly because he had not eaten, partly because he had been upset by what Oates had told him. It was odd, he had hardly considered the risk that he might be tracked down and caught, he had feared only that he might give himself away. He had seen the extra police patrols, the crime cars and the pandas and he knew that all this organisation was for him but he had not once felt threatened. Why should he? All his life he had been on the side of the law and he found it impossible to accept that this had fundamentally changed. But Oates' news had shaken him. He remembered the ring at the doorbell which he had ignored. What would have happened if he had gone down—totally unprepared?

He decide that he would go to the flat, get something to eat and go out again. It was a short distance away.

As he came out of the lift on the top floor he could hear a television newsreader—something about a pay claim for engineering workers. Alice was sitting on the settee, knitting.

'Hullo! You're early. Albert's gone down to set the time switch.' She turned to look at him. 'What's the matter, Jim? Still feeling seedy?'

'I'm all right.'

Her kindly, rather stupid face, expressed concern. 'You don't look it, you . . . '

The newsreader went on, 'This afternoon police made house-to-house enquiries in the Rhynton district of the city. A spokesman said that an un-named man had telephoned Detective Chief Superintendent Wycliffe from a call-box in that neighbourhood this morning.'

'They rang you here.'

'What?'

'The police rang you here, they said there was no answer at the house and a neighbour told them you were living here . . . What's the matter?'

He made a tremendous effort of control. 'You should have told me.'

'You don't give me a chance. Anyway, it's not important. They said it was just routine enquiry, just to find out where everybody was. You really do look poorly, Jim.'

His legs had all but given way and he had dropped into one of the easy chairs. 'I must admit I don't feel so good, I didn't bother with getting any lunch.'

This was a problem Alice could cope with. She bustled through into the kitchen and called to him through the hatch.

'You must have been out.'

'What?'

'When the police called at the house.'

'Yes, I went for a walk. What did they want to know when they telephoned?'

'Nothing much, just whether you were living with us and where you were.'

'What did you say?'

'That you'd gone over to the house as you did every Sunday to give it an airing and they must have missed you.'

'That was all?'

'Yes.'

He felt a little better. If anything it might tend to put them off. Looked at from their point of view it would seem normal—it *was* normal.

Alice brought him a plate of cold meat, some crusty bread and a glass of beer. It put new life into him.

'You're not going out again?'

'I told Jack Oates I would meet him for a drink.'

'But you're not fit, Jim!'

She was genuinely concerned, she was his sister but she meant nothing to him. All the love and affection of which he was capable had been focused on his wife and his daughter. The three of us. No need for anyone else.

He put on his overcoat once more and felt in the right-hand pocket.

The weather had undergone an abrupt change. Instead of the clear, cold frosty night which had promised it had suddenly softened. The air seemed mild and a thick mist diffused through the streets. He walked briskly away from the city centre.

There were few people about and as he got clear of the city centre he had the impression that police patrols were more numerous and obtrusive than on previous nights. He felt that he was being watched. Now and then a patrol car cruised slowly past and twice he came upon police cars parked at intersections. He was climbing a steepish hill out of the city with residential roads off on either side, semi-detached properties with tiny front gardens and narrow strips of sour soil at the back. Rather dreary Edwardian houses which had been the homes of prosperous shop-keepers and tradesmen before the first war; families able to support a couple of maids.

Dorothy Coleman lived in Poulton Avenue which was one of these roads near the top of the hill. As he turned off a police car passed him at little more than walking speed. But nothing now would put him off, he was committed. It was almost as though he had surrendered his will to external compulsion. Twice before he had known the feeling. After spells of torturing doubt his resolution seemed to form and harden of itself.

On the third or fourth gate along the road he could read by the light of a street lamp, a white painted sign:

*Poulton Avenue Nursery School*
*Proprietors: Misses D. Coleman and J. Carter*

There was a light in an upstairs room but none on the ground floor. The little front garden had been paved over. He rang the doorbell and after a moment a light flicked on behind the coloured panes of the front door which was then opened.

She was small and thin—thinner than he remembered, with close-cropped brown hair which made her face look smaller and sharper than it was.

'Miss Coleman?'

She looked up at him through thick lenses. 'Yes, and you must be Mr Grant. Please come in.' She had a rather harsh, metallic voice which must have carried without effort across many classrooms.

He refused her offer to take his coat.

'The school is here on the ground floor, I have a flat upstairs.'

The hall was bare and there was a faint smell of disinfectant but the stairs were carpeted. 'If you would like to come up to the flat we can discuss arrangements and you shall see the school afterwards if you wish.'

He followed her up to a landing and in to the front room. It was a cross between a sitting room and an office; a chesterfield and easies, an old fashioned rolltop desk. There were photographs everywhere, college groups, school groups and half a dozen large paintings in gilt frames—seascapes.

'Won't you sit down?'

He smiled vaguely but remained standing.

'About your grandchild . . .'

'Linda—yes. She is three and a half.' He was well rehearsed. 'My daughter divorced her husband . . .' He told a credible story, his voice was steady, normal. She made sympathetic noises.

187

'I know how difficult it is for a mother who has to work to keep herself and her child but our fees are not high. Will your daughter want Linda to come for the whole day or only part of it?'

He was still standing, showing some interest in the pictures. She seemed vaguely uneasy perhaps because of his refusal to sit down. His hand in the right-hand pocket of his raincoat felt the smooth wooden toggles which he had carved himself.

He made remarks about the pictures expecting that she would join him to point out their merits but she kept her distance. 'They were painted by my father; he made quite a reputation for himself at one time.'

He was patient. No false moves. But they were running out of conversation.

'I expect you would like to see the school?'

'If I may.'

She led the way downstairs and into a room off the hall. A large room, the original dining and drawing rooms knocked into one. Little tables and chairs, an elaborate climbing frame, a magnificent rocking-horse and open shelves all round stacked with books and toys. Lively murals on the walls.

'Our rest room is through here.' A smaller room with mattresses on low wooden frames.

'In the garden we have a toddler's adventure playground.'

He murmured approval and watched her every move. 'Very nice, very suitable. I'm sure my daughter will be delighted.' They were back in the main room and it seemed that his chance would never come but he must not take any risk. Then she darted in front of him and stooped to pick up a plastic cup from the floor which some child had dropped there. In an instant he had the cord out of his pocket. No fumbling. As she straightened, with her back to him, he twisted the nylon cord round her neck and pulled on the toggles with all his strength. She let out a scream which was cut off in a

188

fraction of a second. He had heard a similar scream once before, the girl Bennett had screamed but the first one had made no sound.

She struggled weakly, briefly, then went limp. He held the tension until his forehead was beaded with sweat then he released her. She slipped to the floor and lay sprawled and twisted, her head resting on a rocker of the big toy horse.

His heart thumped unbearably and he could feel a powerful pulse in his neck, his head swam and he was afraid that he might collapse on the floor beside her but the faintness passed.

He stooped to recover the cord and was forced to look at her face. Her eyes were wide open and staring; she looked astonished and, perhaps because her jaw sagged, rather stupid. Her glasses had fallen off. He remembered her expression nine years ago when she had said, 'The trouble with Jane is that she has been spoiled, she is a self-indulgent child and it is high time that she grew up!'

He felt no pity.

As he recovered himself a little he looked round the room to see if he had left any trace of his visit and only then did he realise that the curtains had not been drawn. He was standing in the middle of a lighted room and all that had happened might have been seen by a passer by or even by someone in the houses opposite. At this moment they might be telephoning the police. He walked to the door and switched off the light, the hall light too; then he sat on the stairs in the darkness, he needed a little more time. At last he felt calm enough to leave. He made himself move slowly and deliberately. He let himself out by the front door and shut it behind him. He stood for a moment, listening for footsteps or the sound of a car but there was nothing and he walked to the gate; he closed and latched the gate behind him. Only once more. He would not allow himself to think about that. It was of no importance

189

anyway. He had subordinated himself, forced himself to become an instrument, a tool, and when a tool has served its purpose . . .

Wycliffe felt cold inside.

'I think that we should search the house.'

She looked vague then frightened.

'What's on the top floor?'

'What? Oh, only two attics—lumber rooms, we never go up there.'

'We'll leave those for the moment.' By talking he hoped to get her co-operation without any panic. 'This floor first, you show me.'

The first floor was a self-contained flat, kitchen, bathroom, two bedrooms and the room they had just left. Nothing remarkable except that it was obvious neither of the women had much idea about housekeeping. All the rooms were untidy and looked as though they could do with a good clean.

'Downstairs?'

'All the rooms downstairs and the garden are given over to the school.'

Wycliffe led the way downstairs and opened a door on the left of the hall.

'That's the main schoolroom.'

The room was in darkness and he fumbled for the light switch. When he found it yellow light from a small bulb lit up a large, rather bare room with toddler's tables and chairs and toys scattered about.

It was a moment before he saw her body. She was lying on the floor, her head resting on the blue-painted rocker of a magnificent rocking-horse. Miss Carter saw her at almost the same instant; she let out a gasp but made no other sound. She made no move to enter the room but stood in the doorway, staring, her fist thrust between her teeth like a little girl.

Wycliffe bent over the body but it was obvious that nothing could be done; the strangler was thorough.

Wycliffe went out into the hall and closed the door of the schoolroom behind him.

'Are you all right?'

Miss Carter nodded but she did not remove her hand from her mouth. Wycliffe piloted her gently up the stairs to the sitting room and persuaded her to sit down.

'Would you like something? Tea?'

She shook her head and he went to the telephone. He was put through to Gill.

'I've found her. You'd better get the lads out here and let Franks know. 6 Poulton Avenue—the nursery school . . . No, I shall stay here for the moment. I've got another job for you. Did you get a description from the sister . . . and a photograph? Good! All your mobiles—I want every pub in the city visited beginning with the city centre. They won't have a photograph but they will have the description. Get them moving, Jimmy.'

At first, as he walked, he looked nervously about him but soon he seemed to regain confidence and his whole bearing changed, he stepped out briskly and looked neither to the right nor the left. It was raining, a thin misty drizzle and though from the hill there was a view right across the city he could see only a suffused, angry glow in the sky.

By the time he reached the city centre his mood was buoyant, he felt pleased with himself. For the third time he had not flinched from a dangerous, difficult and horrifying task. He had made a plan and he had carried it through—to the letter. He had been competent that was the word.

He tried never to think of the girl on the allotments, the girl he had nearly killed by mistake. He wanted to blot out that memory because of the guilt he felt, the sense of guilt which had made him so quick to defend himself in the newspaper. A psychopathic killer they had called him. The accusation had frightened him because it was not only, or even mainly his mistaken attack on an innocent girl which made him feel guilty, it was the fact that he had wanted to go on, to finish what he had begun. When the girl's hat had fallen off and he had seen the blond hair it had taken every scrap of will power he possessed to release her. He had known the urge, almost the compulsion to kill. And he had scurried off to the flat and strangled his real victim in a frightening explosion of lust without any plan and at terrible risk.

But in his good times, as now, he could believe that what he had done had been deliberate, a rational and sensible change of plan made necessary by circumstances outside his control.

Once more and it would be over.

He was tempted to finish the thing tonight but he knew that he must resist that kind of prompting. To be competent you had to be calm, that was his secret, and he realised that he was not calm now. He was excited, pleasurably but dangerously so.

But there was no question of going back to the flat—not yet. He walked on through the city centre. A wet Sunday evening and hardly anybody about. Without consciously directing his steps he found himself in Prince's Street. He liked Prince's Street after dark, it seemed to have a teeming life of its own which went on just below the surface. A life which was no more than hinted at by the furtive figures in doorways or by the girls who accosted any unaccompanied male. Now and then between the shops there was an open door into dimly lit passage and a mysterious stairway.

He walked along the pavement with a seemingly purposive stride but in fact he was looking hopefully into every doorway. At the Joiners he went in for a drink. The bar was crowded, full of noise and tobacco smoke and he had to elbow his way to the counter. But, as usual, he seemed to be invisible to the bar-girls until someone said, 'This chap was before me.' Then he ordered a whisky though he rarely drank spirits. He retreated with his drink through the crowd to a clearer space by the windows where there were marble-topped tables. It was there that he saw her, sitting with a gin glass in front of her, showing a great deal of thigh. Her pallor was striking and the great dark eyes in her thin face semed to have a monopoly of all her vitality. She sat, staring at the blank window, apparently unaware of her surroundings. Then she looked up and caught him watching her. Automatically and with scarcely any change of expression she put out her invitation and with equal inevitability he accepted. They were separated by several yards and neither had spoken. The encounter suited his mood, he could play with fire without getting burnt.

He went over to her table. 'Can I get you another drink?'

She glanced back at the crowd round the bar and shook her head. 'It's not worth it.' She stood up, adjusted her shoulder bag and said quietly, 'Just round the corner. Number nine. Open the door and go straight up the stairs.'

He was tremulous with excitement. 'Can't I walk with you?'

She looked at him in surprise. 'No skin off my nose, love, but what if your wife gets to hear of it?'

'I haven't a wife.'

She shrugged. 'Suit yourself.'

She walked quickly with small steps, her heels tapping on the paving stones. He held her arm, thin and rigid through the material of her coat sleeve. He had difficulty in adjusting his pace. It was the first time he had walked out with a woman since . . .

He was silent because he could not trust himself to speak. He had never been with another woman, only with Rose. When he married her at 25 he was a virgin, as she was. Before he married, during the war, he had had the same temptations, the same opportunities as other men but fastidiousness and fear had combined to restrain him. Now for years he had lived like a monk while he watched Rose sink deeper and deeper into depression. But suddenly he was free, unshackled, there was no longer the slightest reason for restraint. He had nothing to fear and nothing to lose.

They turned into number nine. She pushed open the front door and as they entered the little hall she saw him eyeing the door of the bottom flat which was closed.

'What's the matter?'

'Is there another girl in there?'

'She laughed. 'Why? Isn't one enough for you?'

She started up the stairs and he followed. 'Aren't you nervous, going with strange men?'

'No good to be, is it?'

She led him into a bedroom where a gas fire was burning. The room looked homely and cheerful, her dressing gown was on the bed and her make-up and toilet things were spread out on the dressing table.

She had taken off her coat and was hanging it in the wardrobe. 'Four pounds, love.'

He took the notes from his wallet and handed them to her. He stammered. 'I'll give you more if . . . '

She gave him a hard look. 'If what? You're not kinky, are you?'

'No, of course not! I meant if you are . . .' He hesitated, then added, 'if you are nice to me.'

She looked doubtful but she smiled. 'We'll see.' She had put the money in a drawer and taken off her dress. Her skin was white as paper. He watched her, fascinated by her very indifference.

'Aren't you going to undress? How many times had she said those words?

He started to do so. It had not occurred to him that his attraction to this girl sprang from her resemblance to Rose. Rose as she was twenty years ago when Jane was still a little girl. His approaches to Rose had always

194

been tentative, hesitant, her gentle smiling submissiveness disarmed lust and filled him with tenderness. This prostitute, lying naked on her bed, her legs separated waiting for him, had the same effect. She saw the change in him.

'What's the matter? Can't you do it? Come here, I'll help you.'

'No.'

He came to her nevertheless and covered her body with his. He stared down into her eyes and his gaze troubled her for it expressed none of the emotions she was accustomed to read in the faces of men. He looked puzzled as though he had suddenly found something which it was very difficult to explain or understand.

'What's the matter?'

He was caressing her pale face with his hands. His thumbs ran gently down the line of her jaw on either side. It was something he remembered from long ago. His thumbs moved down the throat to where he could feel the gentle pulsing of her blood.

'Oh, Rose!'

'What are you talking about? I aren't called Rose, my name is Brenda.' She saw a change in his expression and was frightened. 'Here! What are you doing? Lay off that!' Then she screamed.

There were heavy footsteps racing up the stairs and a policeman burst into the room.

'All right, dad, we've been looking for you.'

He made no protest but started to dress without a word.

'You all right, love?'

She was sitting on the foot of the bed staring at the man, and, suddenly she started to tremble. The constable put her dressing gown round her shoulders. 'Go into the other room, love, and make yourself a hot drink. He didn't hurt you, did he?'

She shook her head. 'No.' Then she added, 'How did you know?'

'We've been looking for him and they told me in the Joiners you'd picked him up.'

In a very few minutes they were gone and she was left alone.

# CHAPTER ELEVEN

Wycliffe talked to him in an interview room at head-quarters. A little room with pale green walls, brown linoleum on the floor and furnished with a table and two chairs. Wycliffe sat on one side of the table and Rendell on the other; a constable stood by the door.

'Do you smoke?'

'No, thank you.'

'Do you want to make a statement?'

'I don't know. I would rather you asked me questions.'

'In any case I must caution you.' He repeated the formula.

'How long since you had any food?'

'I don't know but I couldn't eat anything.'

'A cup of tea?'

'No, thank you.'

Rendell was 53 but he looked 60. His hair, thin on top, was uniformly grey, his features were deeply lined and he had a whitish stubble on his chin. His skin looked grey and bloodless. His eyes stared unfocused at the table top and his hands rested palms down.

'Would I have killed her?' He asked the question apologetically.

'At any rate, you didn't, you did her no harm other than shock.'

197

'But would I have killed her if—?'

'Perhaps.'

He smoothed the table top with his palms. 'It's been like a nightmare, haunting me. I could never be sure.'

'Of what?'

He glanced up quickly, surprised by the question. 'It's still Sunday, isn't it?'

'A quarter to eleven on Sunday evening.'

He nodded. 'It doesn't seem possible.'

Wycliffe took out his pipe and lit it.

'The newspapers said that I was a psychopathic killer.'

'And you said, "It is not true. If I had been I would have killed the wrong girl on Monday night".'

He stopped moving his hands and focused his eyes on them as though seeing them for the first time. They were well-formed hands, broad and powerful with blunt fingers. Fine brownish-grey hairs glistened in the light.

'But I nearly did kill her.'

'You stopped when her hat fell off and you saw that she had fair hair instead of dark. You realised that she was the wrong girl.'

He nodded several times and was silent for a while. 'Yes, I did stop, didn't I?' He clenched his hands. 'But I wanted to kill her, I don't know how I found the strength to stop. I wanted to kill her even after I knew.'

Wycliffe said nothing, he sat immobile, smoking his pipe in very gentle puffs.

'I didn't understand, you see.'

'What didn't you understand?'

'That it's like sex.'

There was a clock on the wall and every half-minute it made a loud click when the large hand leapt forward a little way. It seemed to distract Rendell, almost to frighten him and he moved his chair so that the clock was no longer in his line of vision.

'It was all so clear in the beginning. I had to punish

the ones who killed my child and my wife. It was my duty.' He stopped, dissatisfied with what he had just said. 'No, it was more than that, I can't explain. It was something I *had* to do, I couldn't help myself.' He looked up at Wycliffe's face to see if he had made himself understood and met the bland impassive stare. 'I'm not trying to excuse myself, I *wanted* to do it, I knew it was right.'

'How did they kill your child and your wife?'

He seemed to think about the question for some time before answering. 'There never was a closer family than we were. We did everything together, the three of us. Of course, I had my work and Jane went to school but what I mean is, our lives centred on each other and on our home.'

'Where did Jane go to school?'

'It was a Catholic school but they took non-Catholics. It's closed now, The School of the Sacred Heart. We wanted her to be with girls who had had a good up-bringing.

'It all started when she went away to that hostel with a lot of girls from other schools. We thought we ought to let her mix more. I find it difficult to tell you how they treated her there.' His voice faltered.

'I know about that.'

'She was never the same. A year later she was in a mental hospital. They said she had mental illness which sometimes affects young people.'

An eavesdropper could have imagined that he was outside a confessional. The subdued, continuing murmur of one voice, the occasional interjections from the priest.

'She came out after six months but she wasn't cured. She was on drugs and she wasn't our Jane any longer. Sometimes she treated us as though we were strangers, she would talk to us but a lot of it was nonsense, she would get her words wrong and her ideas all mixed up.

'She didn't get better, she got worse and they wanted

199

to have her back in hospital, but we wouldn't agree. I can't explain what she was like, she seemed to be cut off, we couldn't reach her. It went on for four years, she was twenty-one but we couldn't let her out of our sight, somebody had to be with her almost all the time. Not that we minded . . . '

He placed his palms together, carefully matching the fingers. 'She seemed to just fade away, physically and mentally, regression I think they called it.

'And then, one afternoon while I was at work, Rose slipped out to the corner shop to buy something for tea and Jane must have followed her. She walked straight out of the house in front of a van, never looked right or left.'

'And your wife blamed herself?'

'Yes. Nothing would convince her that she was not responsible.'

He looked round the room vaguely as though not quite sure where he was.

'I can't understand it.'

'What can't you understand?'

He shook his head. 'I'm not a violent man but the girl on the allotments and the woman tonight . . . After I came away from the nursery school I was worried by the way I felt. I had to prove that they were wrong.'

'Who were wrong?'

'The newspapers.'

'What happened to your wife?' The question jolted him out of his line of thought.

'Rose killed herself. They gave her tablets to make her sleep, she was always taking tablets. Then one morning after I'd gone to work she took all she had. I found her when I came home in the evening.'

'That was last July?'

'Yes.' He passed his hand over his thinning hair as though trying to brush away some irritation. 'That evening, after they had taken her away, I saw it all clearly for the first time. Ever since Jane had become ill

I'd been asking myself, "Why? Why should it happen?" and there it was all the time; Jane had told me—she'd told me everything.'

'What had she told you?' The priest would have said, 'Continue, my son.'

'About the three girls and that woman, how they persecuted her. Suddenly it was clear as daylight and I knew what I had to do.'

'You set about finding these people?'

He nodded. 'It took me six months but I did it.' There was a note of pride in his voice.

In the silence which followed the clock jerked forward three more times, the clicks seemed to get louder. The constable at the door cleared his throat and Rendell turned as though surprised to see him there. The silence continued and two or three times Rendell turned to look at the policeman. Finally he said, 'Does he have to be there?'

Wycliffe made a sign and the constable went out closing the door behind him.

Rendell became increasingly restless, twice he put his hand into his inside breast-pocket and withdrew it again.

'You want to show me something?''

Rendell's hand darted with bird-like swiftness and came out with his wallet. He laid it on the table, opened it and extracted a page torn from a small notebook which he placed in front of Wycliffe. The page was dog-eared and creased from constant handling and it contained three lines of meticulous writing:

*A succession of frustrations or sometimes a single, severe frustration leads to a massive withdrawal from reality and sweeping regression.*

The words *single, severe frustration* had been doubly underlined.

'You see? That proves it, doesn't it? I copied that out

201

of an encyclopaedia. Regression, they say there, that's what the doctor said about Jane.'

Wycliffe passed the paper back and Rendell restored it to his wallet with great care as though it were a precious document, but he did not put his wallet away.

He looked Wycliffe straight in the eyes. 'That's true, isn't it?'

'If you took it from a reliable encyclopaedia I suppose it must be.'

He was excited, trembling, so that his fingers fumbled as he searched his wallet a second time. He came up with a piece of paper similar to the first which he handed over.

'I copied that from a book I got out of the library.'

This piece was not dog-eared or creased, it was obviously more recent than the other.

*The schizophrenic reaction is probably not inherent in all human beings. Many authorities believe that it cannot occur in the absence of certain hereditary factors.*

Rendell was watching him with extraordinary intensity as he read.

'Well?'

'There are many different kinds of mental illness.'

'Schizophrenia, that's what they said it was. I read it in the letter they gave me to give to our doctor. Hebephrenic schizophrenia.'

Wycliffe's placidity was beginning to irritate him. 'Can't you see what it means?'

Wycliffe was treading warily. 'I think I understand what it means but I'm not sure what interpretation you are putting on it.'

Rendell was rocking on his chair with impatience. 'If it's true that it's hereditary then I'm to blame.'

'For what?'

'For everything! I kill for the sake of killing, I'm a

madman like the papers said and I fathered a child who through no fault of her own . . .'

'Rubbish!'

The word and the manner in which it was spoken stopped him like a blow. He quietened down.

'Why did you want to kill the prostitute?'

The abrupt change caught him off balance as Wycliffe intended that it should.

'Why? I don't know.'

'You always have a reason for what you do.'

He thought about that. 'Yes, I do. You are right.' His brow furrowed in an effort of concentration. 'She was dark and thin and pale—like Rose.'

'Did you want to kill Rose?'

A spasm of anger quickly evaporated. 'No! For God's sake, why should I want to kill my wife?'

Wycliffe waited, knowing that the explanation—the rationalisation—would come.

'She lay there waiting for me—resigned. Ready to give me what I had paid for.'

'Well?'

He hesitated for some time then he said in a low voice. 'Rose submitted because she was my wife. She never uttered a word of complaint but . . .

'Each time I vowed I would never make any more demands on her. I felt like a beast. But it's something you can't always control, the situation is there and before you know where you are . . . ' After a moment he added, 'Now they will lock me up and I shan't be able to kill anybody again.' He said the words as though they contained inestimable comfort.

Wycliffe went up to his office and stood by the window in the darkness. He was trying to come to terms with himself. Why had he subjected this man to an interrogation which served no recognised professional end? Out of curiosity? If that meant that he needed to understand. Surely that was more important

than knowing about the electrostatic detection of footprints or the latest methods of recording and analysing
the statistics of crime.

The telephone rang and he groped for it briefly.
'Wycliffe.'

It was Gill. 'So it's all over?'

'They will say that he's unfit to plead.'

'I told you; he's a nutter. They're all the same.'

**THE END**

## WYCLIFFE AND THE BEALES
by W.J. Burley

The village of Washford lay in Hound of the Baskervilles country – but when someone shot the village lay-about, Bunny Newcombe, with a Beretta, everyone was astonished. Who could have done such a thing in their quiet English Village?

Chief Superintendent Wycliffe began to ask his gentle questions and found – constantly – that the answers led him back to Ashill House, home of the Beales, a strange, secretive family of eccentrics and odd-balls. But before Wycliffe could unearth the Beales' family skeleton a second murder followed – and a third murder struck at the very heart of the Beale family itself.

0 552 13232 2

## WYCLIFFE AND THE DEAD FLAUTIST
by W.J. Burley

On the secluded estate of Lord and Lady Bottrel, the body of amateur flautist Tony Mills was found, shot by his own gun – apparently suicide. But a closer examination revealed some rather sinister inconsistencies and Chief Superintendent Wycliffe was called in.

As he began to unravel the last days of the dead man, another mystery was revealed – the disappearance of Lizzie Biddick, pretty young maid at the Bottrel ancestral home. Gradually bitter family feuds and secret illicit relationships were uncovered, and then another body was found, shattering for ever the pastoral peace of the Cornish Estate.

0 552 14264 6

## WYCLIFFE AND THE TANGLED WEB
by W.J. Burley

Hilda Clemo, bright, beautiful, still at school, dropped the bombshell of her pregnancy to her family and boyfriend – and then vanished from her Cornish village that same summer afternoon. As fears for her safety grew, Chief Superintendent Wycliffe was brought in to search the fields and cliffs and question the Clemo family – a weird, feuding clan whose kinship and hatreds covered some unpleasant secrets.

One of the secrets finally led to the discovery of a body – but not the body of Hilda Clemo. By the time Hilda's corpse was found, Wycliffe had a welter of mysteries to solve, not least the true character of the precocious murdered schoolgirl.

0 552 14268 9

## WYCLIFFE AND THE QUIET VIRGIN
by W.J. Burley

Mynhager House, high on the cliffs overlooking the sea, was a gray and forbidding place as Wycliffe arrived to spend the Christmas holiday with a friend. And the festive season proved to be anything but festive as, first the 'Virgin' in the local Nativity play – a sexy teenager called Francine – vanished into thin air. Then her mother, a beautiful but melancholy woman was found dead, shot through the skull.

As corpse followed corpse, Wycliffe found himself uncovering a cauldron of corruption, blackmail, and long-buried secrets of passion. And most of the secrets – the clues to the present murders – seemed to stem from Mynhanger House, the home of his friend and host.

0 552 13435 X

## WYCLIFFE AND THE SCAPEGOAT
by W.J. Burley

Each year, at Hallowe'en, high on the Cornish cliffs, a life-sized effigy of a man was strapped to a blazing wheel and run into the sea – a re-enactment of a hideous old legend where the figure had been a living sacrifice.

And now Jonathan Riddle, a well-known and respected local builder and undertaker, had disappeared, and it seemed all too likely that his corpse had gone the way of the historic 'scapegoat'.

As Chief Superintendent Wycliffe began to investigate the family life of Riddle, more and more unpleasant facts began to emerge until he was left with an incredible and seemingly impossible solution.

0 552 14266 2

## WYCLIFFE AND THE WINSOR BLUE
by W.J. Burley

When Edwin Garland died of a heart attack, no one outside the expectant circle of his relatives was concerned. But when, on the evening of his funeral, his son was shot dead, the situation changed dramatically and Superintendent Wycliffe was called in to investigate the seemingly motiveless murder.

The disappearance of another relative and further death occur before Wycliffe manages to unravel a story that had begun several years before, with the death of a famous Cornish artist. Only then is he able to identify the killer.

0 552 13436 8

# A SELECTED LIST OF CRIME NOVELS
# AVAILABLE FROM CORGI BOOKS

THE PRICES SHOWN BELOW WERE CORRECT AT THE TIME OF GOING TO PRESS.
HOWEVER TRANSWORLD PUBLISHERS RESERVE THE RIGHT TO SHOW NEW RETAIL
PRICES ON COVERS WHICH MAY DIFFER FROM THOSE PREVIOUSLY ADVERTISED IN
THE TEXT OR ELSEWHERE.

| | | | | |
|---|---|---|---|---|
| ☑ | 13232 2 | WYCLIFFE AND THE BEALES | W.J. Burley | £3.99 |
| ☐ | 14264 6 | WYCLIFFE AND THE DEAD FLAUTIST | W.J. Burley | £3.99 |
| ☑ | 14221 2 | WYCLIFFE AND THE DUNES MYSTERY | W.J. Burley | £3.99 |
| ☑ | 14268 9 | WYCLIFFE AND THE TANGLED WEB | W.J. Burley | £3.99 |
| ☑ | 14109 7 | WYCLIFFE AND THE CYCLE OF DEATH | W.J. Burley | £3.99 |
| ☑ | 13689 1 | WYCLIFFE AND DEATH IN STANLEY STREET | W.J. Burley | £3.99 |
| ☑ | 14267 0 | WYCLIFFE AND THE FOUR JACKS | W.J. Burley | £3.99 |
| ☐ | 13435 X | WYCLIFFE AND THE QUIET VIRGIN | W.J. Burley | £3.99 |
| ☑ | 14266 2 | WYCLIFFE AND THE SCAPEGOAT | W.J. Burley | £3.99 |
| ☑ | 14269 7 | WYCLIFFE'S WILD-GOOSE CHASE | W.J. Burley | £3.99 |
| ☐ | 13436 8 | WYCLIFFE AND THE WINSOR BLUE | W.J. Burley | £3.99 |
| ☑ | 13433 3 | WYCLIFFE IN PAUL'S COURT | W.J. Burley | £3.99 |
| ☐ | 12804 X | WYCLIFFE AND THE PEA-GREEN BOAT | W.J. Burley | £3.99 |
| ☑ | 14265 4 | WYCLIFFE AND THE LAST RITES | W.J. Burley | £3.99 |
| ☑ | 14117 8 | WYCLIFFE AND HOW TO KILL A CAT | W.J. Burley | £3.99 |
| ☑ | 14115 1 | WYCLIFFE AND THE GUILT EDGED ALIBI | W.J. Burley | £3.99 |
| ☑ | 14205 0 | WYCLIFFE AND THE THREE-TOED PUSSY | W.J. Burley | £3.99 |
| ☑ | 14116 X | WYCLIFFE AND DEATH IN A SALUBRIOUS PLACE | W.J. Burley | £3.99 |
| ☑ | 14437 1 | WYCLIFFE AND THE HOUSE OF FEAR | W.J. Burley | £3.99 |
| ☐ | 14295 6 | A CLEAR CONSCIENCE | Frances Fyfield | £4.99 |
| ☐ | 14043 0 | SHADOW PLAY | Frances Fyfield | £4.99 |
| ☐ | 14174 7 | PERFECTLY PURE AND GOOD | Frances Fyfield | £4.99 |
| ☐ | 13840 1 | CLOSED CIRCLE | Robert Goddard | £5.99 |
| ☐ | 13839 8 | HAND IN GLOVE | Robert Goddard | £5.99 |
| ☐ | 13281 0 | IN PALE BATTALIONS | Robert Goddard | £4.99 |
| ☐ | 13982 3 | A TOUCH OF FROST | R.D. Wingfield | £4.99 |
| ☐ | 13981 5 | FROST AT CHRISTMAS | R.D. Wingfield | £5.99 |
| ☐ | 13985 8 | NIGHT FROST | R.D. Wingfield | £4.99 |
| ☐ | 14409 6 | HARD FROST | R.D. Wingfield | £5.99 |

All Transworld titles are available by post from:

**Book Service By Post, PO Box 29, Douglas, Isle of Man IM99 1BQ**

Credit cards accepted. Please telephone 01624 675137, fax 01624 670923 or
Internet http://www.bookpost.co.uk for details.

Please allow £0.75 per book for post and packing UK.
Overseas customers allow £1 per book for post and packing.